PLANTS VS. ZOMBIES™

PLANT YOUR PATH

Junior Novel

by Tracey West

HARPER FESTIVAL
An Imprint of HarperCollinsPublishers

HarperFestival
is an imprint
of HarperCollins
Publishers.

Plants vs. Zombies:
Plant Your Path Junior Novel
Text and illustration © 2014 by Electronic Arts Inc.
Plants vs. Zombies is a trademark of Electronic Arts Inc.
www.harpercollinschildrens.com
Library of Congress catalog card number: 2013951750
ISBN 978-0-06-229494-4
Book design by Victor Joseph Ochoa

14 15 16 17 OPM 10 9 8 7 6 5

❖

First Edition

Get Ready to Soil Your Plants!

So you're probably wondering . . . why do I need instructions for reading this book? I just start at the middle and keep reading until the end, right?

Wrong! This is no ordinary book. It's a Plant Your Path novel, which means you get to choose what happens in the story by picking the path that you take. When you come to a choice, pick one and go to that page. But be careful . . . you might end up saving the day or the zombies might end up eating your brains.

And if you don't like the story that sprouts? No biggie. Just go back to where you started and choose a different path, and you'll get a different story. It's like a Sunflower that keeps giving you more sun! Only instead of sun, you get nonstop action. So what are you waiting for? Get growing!

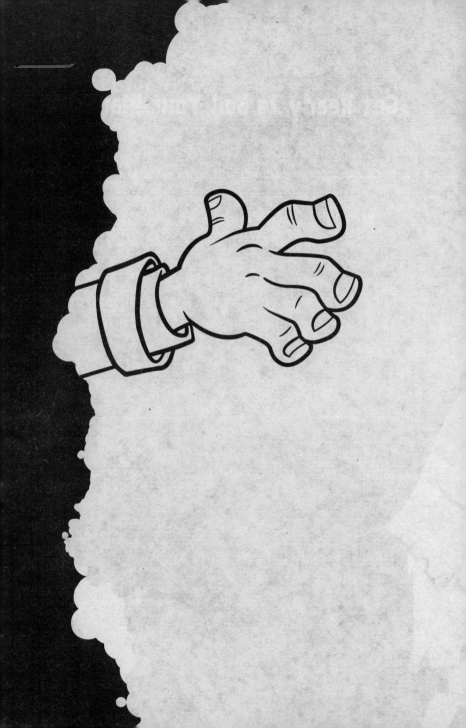

It's a sunny Saturday afternoon, and your parents are out taking ballroom dancing lessons. Normally they'd be telling you to clean your room or take out the garbage, and you were looking forward to a peaceful day to yourself, lounging by the pool in your backyard. Except . . .

Ding-dong! The doorbell rings, and you open the front door. There, standing on your front step, are Matt and Emma. They're both in your grade in school, but they're not really friends. Fate has brought you together today—actually, it was Mrs. Buckworth, your science teacher. She's grouped you together for your science project.

If you looked up "high school football player" in the dictionary, you'd probably see a picture of Matt. He's as tall as a small tree with bulky muscles and perfectly trimmed short brown hair. He's wearing his black-and-gold team jersey with the number 35 on it.

"Yo," he says, when he steps into your house.

"Um, yo," you say, a little awkwardly. The only football you've ever played has been in video games.

Then there's Emma. She's in the drama club and has thick black hair with bangs across her forehead. She's wearing bright pink sneakers, black skinny jeans, and a T-shirt with "Broadway Bound" written across it in glittery letters. Silver star earrings dangle from her ears.

"What's with all the lawn mowers?" she asks, with a nod to your lawn. It's a perfect square of trimmed green grass, and four lawn mowers are neatly lined up in front of the house, facing the lawn. The only plant on the lawn is a Peashooter, a little green plant with a bulb-shaped flower and two cute little black eyes.

"My mom is a lawn freak," you explain. "She's like, constantly mowing the lawn."

Emma nods, like it's the most normal thing in

the world. Matt pushes past you.

"Can we get this over with?" he asks. "I've got practice in a few hours."

"And I've got an audition," Emma says, with a toss of her black hair. "It's community theater." She says it like it's important.

You motion for them to follow you into the kitchen, and you all sit around the table. "Fine by me. We just need to decide on our project today, and like, write a page about it."

"I've got the perfect thing," Matt says. "It's Biology class, right? So we do sports nutrition. Like, how food affects your cells and stuff. Do you have anything to eat?"

"Oh, sure," you say, getting up and grabbing a bunch of bananas from the counter. "But I was thinking—"

"We should do something about the biology of *emotions*," Emma said. "You know, like we could measure our subjects' heart rates when they're angry, or sad, or excited."

"That's cool," you say. "But I was thinking more about plant biology."

"Plants are boring," said Matt, stuffing a banana into his mouth.

"Well, they're not, really," you say. "I have this neighbor, Crazy Dave, and—"

Bam! A guy wearing a pot on his head bursts through your back door. He has a bushy beard and mustache; his eyes are looking in two different directions; and his white polo shirt is riding up on his wobbly belly.

"Flobble hurfle! Wabbo wimbo! Zombies!"

"Oh, hi, Crazy Dave," you say.

Matt jumps up and strikes a karate pose. "Back off, weird dude!"

"He's okay," you assure him. "Crazy Dave is harmless."

"Wah-WEE-oh!" Crazy Dave yells.

"He looks kind of upset," Emma says, eyeing Crazy Dave curiously. "What's he saying?"

You've known Crazy Dave since you were a kid, so you're pretty good at interpreting. "He's saying, 'They're here! Zombies! Lots of zombies!'" you explain. "But he's always talking about zombies. It's no big deal."

Crazy Dave rushes to your chair and picks you up by your shoulders, giving you a shake. Then he puts you down and stomps off toward the front door.

"He seems pretty convinced," Emma remarks,

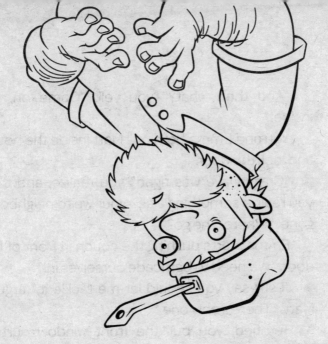

and she rushes off to follow him. A few seconds later, you hear her scream.

You and Matt rush outside. Pale and shaking, Emma is pointing down the street, where a lone zombie is slowly shuffling around the corner. You've never actually seen a real zombie before, but it can't be anything else: It has gray skin, no hair, and a mouth full of crooked teeth. Its eyes are crooked too, and its suit jacket and pants are hanging off its skinny body. It's a zombie, all right.

"Get inside!" Emma yells.

"No, we should take it down!" Matt cries. "Tackle it!"

"And then what?" you yell. "Come on, get inside!"

You and Emma both pull Matt inside the house and lock the door.

"Crazy Dave was right!" you realize, and then you realize something else—your weird neighbor is gone. "Where'd he go?"

Emma starts pushing the couch in front of the door. "We need to barricade ourselves in!"

"I still say you should let me tackle it," argues Matt. "There's only one."

Terrified, you pull the front window curtain aside and peer out. The zombie is crossing the street now, approaching your lawn.

"He knows we're in here!" Emma yells.

That's when you notice little green balls shooting through the air. They're coming from the Peashooter! The balls slam into the zombie's chest again . . . and again . . . and again . . .

"Whoa! That plant is attacking the zombie," Matt says.

Then . . . *poof!* The zombie's head pops off its shoulders and it collapses on the grass.

"Touchdown!" Matt yells, just as Crazy Dave bursts through your front door. He puts a shovel in your hand and motions for you to follow him to your shed in the backyard. He flings open the door and you see a bunch of plants there.

"Moz plobbo bog floodie," he says. "Plap wabby woggy. Sunflowers hoopity hoo!"

"More zombies are coming," you interpret. "Plants will defeat them. Get sun so your plants will sprout fast."

"I see more Peashooter seeds," Emma says, exploring the shed.

Matt picks up a seed packet labeled "Cherry Bomb."

"These have got to be better," Matt says. "We can bomb those zombies to bits!"

If you start out planting Cherry Bombs, go to page 72.

If you plant a row of Peashooters, go to page 122.

Continued from page 107.

The more sun we have, the more plants we can plant," you reason. "So let's buy a Twin Sunflower. You know what they say—two heads are better than one!"

"Unless it's a two-headed zombie," Matt points out.

Your logic is good—except that it's extra sunny up on the roof, and your plants sprout quickly. You don't really need the Twin Sunflower. And you're not prepared for the new zombies that attack you on the roof.

Bungee Zombies drop from the sky to steal your plants. Ladder Zombies rush forward faster than you can stop them. Then an enormous Gargantuar appears, a monstrous zombie with a tiny Imp on its back. It crushes your plants and destroys your defenses.

The zombies climb down your chimney, and there's nothing you can do to stop them now.

THE ZOMBIES EAT YOUR BRAINS!

"Football players like to work out, don't they?" Emma asks. "Maybe Matt's in the gym."

"This far? And without a car?" you ask.

Emma shrugs. "I don't know. It's worth a try."

She pulls up in front of the Mega Muscle Gym. There's a sign out front with a picture of a bodybuilder with huge muscles. Somebody has spray-painted an arrow pointing to his head, with the word, "Brains!"

"Um, guys, I don't think this is such a good idea," you say, but Emma and Crazy Dave have already gone inside.

"Guys, did you see that sign outside?" you call out.

Crazy Dave has found the smoothie machine and is sucking down a pink frozen concoction right from the spout. Emma is looking around.

"Matt? Anybody here?" she calls out.

"Braaaaiiiiiiiiins!"

In response, a small group of zombies bursts from the locker room door.

"Run!" you yell. You pull Crazy Dave away from the smoothie machine and, with Emma, head through the nearest door.

You've reached the indoor pool. Inside, you can see Ducky Tube Zombies paddling in the water and Snorkel Zombies lurking beneath the surface. You turn around, but the zombies from the locker room have followed you inside.

"There's no way out!" Emma screams.

You turn to Crazy Dave. "We have seeds, right?"

"Wibbly pad nope," he replies, pointing to the pool. "Glarb!"

"But no Lily Pads," you translate, sadly. There's no escape. The pot on Crazy Dave's head keeps him safe, but as for you and Emma . . .

THE ZOMBIES EAT YOUR BRAINS!

"Just make this right turn, quick!" you yell.

The wheels screech as Emma turns the car hard to the right. You tear down the paved road, leaving the zombies in your dust.

"Zibby wobba wheresie?" Crazy Dave asks, sticking his big head between you and Emma.

"I'm not sure where we're going," Emma says. "To find Matt. To find somewhere safe. To look for a happy ending."

Crazy Dave shrugs. He settles into the backseat, and then he starts to sing a song about squirbos.

His voice sounds like a cross between a dying bird and a garbage disposal. He motions for you to join him.

You want to keep Crazy Dave happy, so you sing a few verses with him. But by the seventy-ninth squirbo you wish you hadn't. You're starting to think you'd be better off outside the car, facing the zombies alone.

Emma drives . . . and drives . . . and drives. Every once in a while you pass a lone zombie shuffling along the road, but no more hordes. Then before you know it, it starts to get dark.

"Wibby mabo safe place," Crazy Dave says, and you agree.

"You're right. Those buildings up ahead look like a safe place to spend the night," you say, pointing.

Emma slows down so you can check them out. The first building is a convenience store, but it looks abandoned. In the big lot next to it is what looks like a traveling carnival. The big sign over the entrance reads **HAVE FUN AT THE PLANT-O-RAMA!** and there are Sunflowers painted on it.

"Wabby woo," Crazy Dave says excitedly, eyeing the carnival.

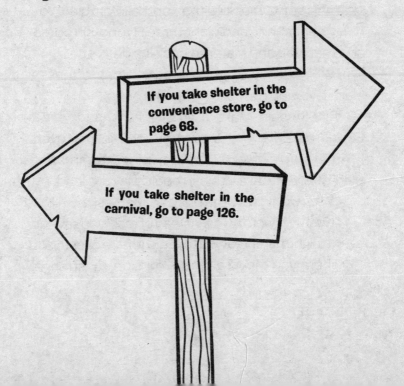

If you take shelter in the convenience store, go to page 68.

If you take shelter in the carnival, go to page 126.

Continued from page 66.

"The Sun-shrooms are giving us enough sun for a few small plants, like the Hypno-shrooms; or for one bigger plant, like the Doom-shroom," you report, looking outside.

"The guide says that if a zombie bites a Hypno-shroom, then the zombie will turn around and attack other zombies," Emma says, looking in the guide.

"Sounds good," you say. "We can plant them on the front lines."

"I'm on defense," Matt says, and rushes outside and starts blocking the Football Zombies. You hurry behind him and plant three Hypno-shrooms, and then you and Matt run back inside.

"Whoa! They've got a pretty strong offense," Matt says, and he looks a little shaky.

"This would make a great play, wouldn't it?" Emma asks, getting a dreamy look in her eyes. "Three people stuck in a house, using their amazing plants to fend off zombies. I could play the lead. . . ."

"Who would play the plants?" Matt asks.

"I wish this were a play, instead of real," you say. "Or even a nightmare. Yeah, I'd take nightmare over this."

Then you hear a noise outside, a strange,

spooky sound that lets you know the Football Zombies are close. You look outside and see that the Hypno-shrooms have sprouted. They have purple-and-pink caps and swirly eyes. One of the Football Zombies is eating a Repeater, but the other two are munching on the Hypno-shrooms. After a few bites, the zombies turn around and attack the third Football Zombie.

"Woo-hoo!" Matt cheers.

The coast is clear for a minute, so you plant another Hypno-shroom and some more Puff-shrooms. It's just in time, because a small team of Football Zombies charges you next. Half of them eat the Hypno-shrooms, and pretty soon they're all attacking each other.

"This is a pretty good game," remarks Matt.

And then it's over, and you realize how exhausted you are.

"We should try to sleep," you say. You get some sleeping bags for Matt and Emma and you head to your own bed. But it's hard to sleep, because you keep dreaming that a zombie is attacking you, and a Peashooter is shooting it over, and over, and over . . .

"Wake up!" Emma says, shaking you. "Look at

what we just found on the front lawn!"

You open your eyes to find sun streaming through your window. Yawning, you read the note:

> We herd you were having a pool party. We think that iz fun. We'll be rite over.
>
> Sincerely,
> The Zombies

You sit straight up. "Oh no! They're going to attack the backyard!"

You race downstairs with Emma at your heels. Matt is calmly eating a bowl of cereal at your table. When you get outside, Crazy Dave is by your shed, waving some seed packets.

"Fnarble gibble swimmin' pool!" he's yelling. "Wubby zummy lippity padses!"

"Plant Lily Pads first, then plant on top of the Lily Pads," you say. "Got it!"

Crazy Dave rushes off, and something falls to the ground behind him. Emma picks it up. "It's a car key," she says, but there's no time to run after

Crazy Dave, so she slips it in her pocket.

Then she stands back and holds up her hands, examining the yard like the director of a movie. "Let's see. You've got this big pool here, with grass on either side. So let's plant some Sunflowers in the lawn and take it from there."

"Matt! Can you help?" you yell back into the house.

Matt jogs out. "Put me in, Coach!"

It seems like the three of you have been fighting zombies together forever, and you come up with a strategy. You plant Sunflowers close to the house, and then some trusty Peashooters in rows in front of them. Then you place Lily Pads on top of the pool.

"Let's get some plants on top of these," you say.

"Crazy Dave gave us a lot of new seeds," Emma says, flipping through the *Suburban Almanac*. "We need to find the right plant for the right zombie. Like finding the right actor for the right role."

"Well, this horror movie's starting again," you say. "Look!"

A slow-moving zombie is the first to shuffle into your backyard, and a Peashooter takes it down. The next few zombies all march onto the grass, moaning and groaning. None seem interested in the pool.

Then a zombie appears wearing an inflatable ducky tube around its waist.

"This guy likes the pool," Emma calls out, reading from the book. "Try a shooter on one of those Lily Pads!"

You place a couple of Peashooters on two Lily Pads and they get to work blasting the Ducky Tube Zombie. You're feeling pretty good until a new zombie appears. This one is wearing a red wetsuit and carrying a dolphin under its arm.

"Should we get more shooters on Lily Pads?" you call out.

"This one's a Dolphin Rider," Emma reports. "It 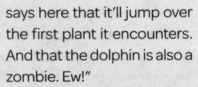 says here that it'll jump over the first plant it encounters. And that the dolphin is also a zombie. Ew!"

"Hmm," you say, looking at the pool. You've got two rows of Lily Pads waiting for plants on top, and Peashooters in the last row. "What other seeds do we have?"

Matt picks up the seed packs. "There's a Squash."

"It takes out a zombie to the left or right of it, but then it's done," Emma reports. "It won't sprout again."

"Anything else?" you ask.

"Tangle Kelp," Matt reports.

"It drags zombies under the water, and then it won't sprout again, either," says Emma.

"Which one needs more sun to sprout?" you ask.

Emma flips through the pages. "Squash. Tangle Kelp hardly needs any."

If you use Tangle Kelp to stop the Dolphin Rider Zombie, go to page 48.

OR

If you use a Squash, go to page 108.

Continued from page 38.

Something Emma says strikes a chord—you're tired of sitting around, waiting for zombies to attack. Going on a zombie hunt sounds like fun.

Crazy Dave frowns. "Bliggy blarf seeds berfer."

"No need, my dear friend, I have plenty of seeds," says Stanley. He goes inside his tent and returns with several seed packets. "Squash, Potato Mine, Cherry Bomb, and Jalapeño."

Stanley has selected seeds that do a lot of damage—and then can't sprout again. Powerful, but you don't get steady power with them.

"Shouldn't we—" you start to say, but Stanley interrupts you.

"No time to waste! Off, my new friends, on our exciting adventure!" he cries. He puts an arm around you and the other around Emma, walking you through the crowd. The survivors look down at their feet, avoiding your eyes.

You look behind you. "See you later, Crazy Dave!"

"Glurb!"

Stanley Stemworth leads you down a path in the forest.

"Are the zombies in these woods?" Emma asks.

"They prefer human haunts," Stanley says. "Several have holed up in an abandoned general store nearby. It contains many foodstuffs and other useful items, such as seeds, but so far we haven't been able to defeat them. We have lost many . . . plants, trying to do so."

Soon the path opens up to a dirt road and a small general store with a wood porch in front.

"So what's the plan?" Emma whispers.

"You two shall act as bait," Stanley whispers back. "And I shall throw some plants in that sunny spot. When the zombies attack, you run back here and let the plants do their work."

Stanley starts to toss seeds into a sunny patch of dirt right outside the door. Soon, you see a Potato Mine sprouting.

Emma's eyes are shining with excitement. "This is the role of a lifetime," she says. "Here I go!"

She marches toward the general store. "What a lovely day it is out here! And how nice it is to feel the sun on my head, which houses my sweet, juicy brains."

Stanley gives you a little push. "Excellent! Now do what she does."

You don't really like the idea of being bait, but you can't leave Emma out there on her own. You slowly walk toward her.

"Um, I've got brains," you say. "Um, really big brains."

It works. A small group of Buckethead Zombies pushes out of the store, stumbling toward you with their arms extended.

"Get back!" Stanley yells.

You and Emma start to run back toward the woods as the plants do their work.

Boom! Bam! Pow! The Potato Mine explodes, and Stanley is throwing out Jalapeños and Cherry Bombs.

Squash! Two grumpy Squash crush two of the Bucketheads instantly.

"It's working!" Stanley cries, clapping his hands.

When the dust clears, you can still see a Buckethead Zombie lurking in the doorway. Then you hear Emma scream. You turn around to see three Screen Door Zombies coming through the woods.

"I thought you said there were no zombies in the woods!" she yells at Stanley.

"Did I? I don't recall," Stanley says, nervously

twiddling his thumbs.

"Plant some more plants!" you yell.

He shows you his empty hands. "I would like to, but I am out of seeds."

You're starting to think that this "fearless leader" isn't so fearless—or much of a leader, either. Your mind races as you try to think of a way to escape the zombie onslaught.

If you run to the nearby swamp, go to page 92.

If you run into the store to find more seeds, go to page 116.

Continued from page 53.

"Let's grab some Cherry Bombs!" you yell, and you and Emma each pluck one off a shelf. The plants are sprouted and ready to go.

You nod to Emma. "Run for the doors!" Then you toss your Cherry Bomb in front of you.

Boom! It explodes, wiping out three zombies as you race across the room. Then Emma tosses hers.

Boom! She takes out four more. But before you can reach the doors, two Pogo Zombies cut across the room, blocking you.

Looking over your shoulder, you see a bunch of zombies shuffling behind you. You're trapped.

"If this were a scene in a movie, somebody would be coming to our rescue right about now," Emma says nervously.

And that's when . . .

"Waaaaaabooooooooooo!"

Crazy Dave bashes down the mechanical door in his car. He barrels through the zombies and skids to a stop in front of you.

"Zibadoo!" he yells, motioning for you to get in.

The two of you quickly jump into the backseat.

You barely have time to close the door before he does a 360 and speeds back out of the room. He tears down the hallway and drives through the front door of the factory, sending glass flying everywhere.

"Thanks, Crazy Dave," you say. "How did you know we were in trouble?"

"Wabbo KABOOM!" your rescuer replies.

Then he punches the gas pedal again, and you're thrown back in your seat. That's when you notice all the stuff he's got in the back of his car. There are seeds for plants you've never seen before, with names like Gatling Pea and Gloom-shroom.

"What's all this?" you ask.

"Flibbo frambo," Crazy Dave says.

"Upgrade plants! We can use them to rescue more people," you say to Emma with a smile. Rescuing people from zombies with Crazy Dave as your leader? That's as much fun as a barrel full of squirbos!

THE END

"The Balloon Zombie is headed straight down the left side of the pool," you say. "Let's plant a row of Cactus there."

Then the Plantern goes out. You can't see the Balloon Zombie anymore, but you think you got the Cactus in a straight line. You stumble through the fog, throwing down three Cactus seeds in a row. Then you head back to the safety of the house.

You patiently wait while the moaning of the zombies grows louder. Then the wind blows and the fog clears . . . and you see that the Balloon Zombie has drifted to the other side of the lawn! There are no Cactus plants on that side to stop it.

Emma jumps up. "I can plant one before it gets to the house!" she cries, picking up the seed packet.

You grab her by the arm. "Emma, it's too dangerous."

She looks you in the eyes. "I have to. I haven't had a big scene yet, and we'll need it when this gets made into a movie."

Then she runs outside just as the fog rolls in again. You're not sure what's happening.

"Dude, throw out a Plantern," Matt suggests.

You do, and in a few seconds the Plantern's light scatters the fog. You see the Balloon Zombie fly right up to a lawn mower parked against your house.

Vroooooooom! The lawn mower starts up and shreds across the lawn, pushing back the Balloon Zombie.

That's the good news. The bad news is . . .

"Emma's gone!" you yell.

If you go look for Emma, go to page 67.

If you stay and fight the zombies, go to page 138.

"Which ones should we use?" you ask, pan-icked.

Crazy Dave shrugs. "Eenie meenie, marfle mocha-cha squirbo in the toe . . ." He finishes the rhyme and holds up the Super-Duper Seeds. "Ta da!"

"Okay, everybody get in a circle!" you yell. The survivors obey, and you start planting the seeds in a circle all around you. The Dancing Zombies are shuffling closer now, dancing to the beat of the eerie disco music.

The seeds sprout, and you're happy to see Sun-shrooms, Puff-shrooms, Fume-shrooms, and Hypno-shrooms. But they don't seem to be doing anything. Their eyes are closed.

"Why aren't they attacking?" you ask.

Emma points to the sun. "It's daytime. We need Coffee Beans to wake them up."

You groan. "We need to plant that other seed packet!"

Then . . . *poof!* Four Backup Dancer Zombies break through the ground around each Dancing Zombie. You don't need to count—you know that the zombies outnumber you.

You throw down the Really Awesome Seeds, but they take too long to sprout. The Dancing Zombies and Backup Dancers descend on you, boogieing to the beat.

"I guess disco will be the death of us," you tell Emma, just as . . .

THE ZOMBIES EAT YOUR BRAINS!

You quickly plant some Magnet-shrooms and wake them up with Coffee Beans. While you're doing that, Crazy Dave fires up a lawn mower and chases away the first Digger Zombie.

"Wabbo!" he yells. But wait, there's more! The earth rumbles and one . . . two . . . three . . . four Digger Zombies march up to your defenses. But the Magnet-shrooms are charged up.

Zip! Zip! Zip! Zip! Four pickaxes go flying through the air, drawn to the Magnet-shrooms. Without their pickaxes, the Digger Zombies can't dig. You can attack them just like regular zombies.

And that's just what your Cob Cannons do. Ears of corn shoot through the air like missiles, taking down all the zombies in the wave.

You lean back, exhausted. "We did it!"

"But who knows when the next attack will be?" Emma points out. "And don't forget, there's a room inside full of zombies trying to get out. We can't save this factory."

Your eye is drawn to a Bloom & Doom delivery truck in the parking lot. "Maybe not, but we can save the seeds."

Crazy Dave's eyes light up. He starts throwing seeds into the back of the truck.

Together, you load the truck with every seed packet you can find. Then you drive away.

The world needs plants, and you've got the seeds. You may be the planet's last hope.

THE END

Continued from page 143.

"That sign looks like it was made by humans," you say. "Maybe they can help us get out of here."

"Sounds good to me," Emma says, and she turns down the road.

There's a thick forest on either side of you. Then the trees open up into a clearing.

Two people jump in front of the car. One is a man wearing overalls and carrying a pitchfork. The other is a woman with long braids who's holding a shovel. They hold out the tools like they're weapons.

"Stop right there!" the woman yells.

Emma slams on the brakes.

The man squints. "They don't look like zombies," he tells the woman.

"We're not!" you yell, sticking your head out of the car. "All alive, see? And we hate brains."

"Get out of the car, slowly," the woman commands.

You, Emma, and Crazy Dave obey. The man and woman get behind you and you feel the prod of a pitchfork in your back.

"Get movin'," the man says.

"Where are you taking us?" Emma asks.

"To our leader," he replies gruffly.

You keep walking, curious, as the couple leads you through a makeshift camp. There are several tents set up, and tarps hung over trees, and campfires burning. Men, women, and children with dirt-streaked faces gather around to get a look at you.

You come to a stop in front of a green tent. There's a crude sign on a stick next to the tent that reads **FEARLESS LEADER**. The tent flap opens and a short, round man with an old-timey mustache steps out.

Crazy Dave rushes up and hugs him.

"Crazy Dave!" the man replies, hugging him back. "Still crazy, I see."

"Wabbo walloo!" Crazy Dave says, and then starts to laugh.

"You know this guy?" you ask Crazy Dave.

Stanley answers. "I'm Stanley Stemworth. Crazy Dave and I studied advanced plantology together in college. We had some good times back then, eh, chum?"

"Blaggo!" Crazy Dave replies.

"So, anyway, what is this place?" you ask.

"We are survivors!" Stanley replies, motioning to the group gathered around. "Our community was destroyed by zombies, so we have fled here. And because I have the most expert knowledge of plants, they have elected me their leader."

"We've been fighting zombies too," Emma says. "We were hoping to find someplace safe from them."

"Fighting zombies, eh?" Stanley says, twirling his mustache. "Then you're just the brai—I mean, people, I've been waiting for. I am organizing a zombie hunt this afternoon. Would you like to join me?"

Crazy Dave grunts disapprovingly.

"I don't know," Emma says. "I'd rather hunt zombies than stick around, waiting to get eaten."

If you decide to go on a zombie hunt with Stanley, go to page 24.

If you convince Emma that you should stay in the camp, go to page 111.

On the seed packet, the Repeaters look like Peashooters, only bigger. The Chomper is a plant with a big purple bulb that opens up to reveal sharp white teeth.

"That Chomper looks awesome," Matt says. He bravely runs out the front door and quickly plants it in a row in front of all the other plants.

As he runs back inside, the Chomper sprouts, and a zombie approaches it.

Gulp! The Chomper swallows the zombie and begins chewing it.

"All right!" you say, high-fiving Matt.

But then two more zombies come up and start chomping on the Chomper. It still has its mouth full, so it can't defend itself.

"You should have planted it behind a Wall-nut!" Emma says.

But it's too late now. A zombie waving a flag marches up, and a huge wave of zombies appears behind him. They eat your Wall-nuts and your Peashooters. Then they burst into your house, and . . .

THE ZOMBIES EAT YOUR BRAINS!

Continued from page 70.

"There could be people down there," Emma says.

"Or zombies," you point out.

"Then bring it on!" Emma says, frustrated. "I mean, we're going nowhere! If there are people there and they can tell us what's going on, I want to find out."

Emma makes a good point. "All right, let's do it," you say.

Emma turns down the road, and it opens up to a paved parking lot in front of a big concrete building. The sign above the entrance reads **BLOOM & DOOM SEED COMPANY**.

That sounds familiar. You take out a seed packet from your backpack and see the same name on the packet.

"This is the company that makes all the seeds!" you say.

Crazy Dave puts down the magazine. His face lights up when he sees the sign on the building.

"Sabble habbadoo!" he says. His eyes are practically spinning, he's so excited.

"Secret headquarters? If there's a safe place,

it's got to be this place, right?" Emma asks, a little nervously.

"Might as well find out," you say.

Crazy Dave is already out of the car and through the front doors. You and Emma follow him in.

"Hello?" you call out, and your voice echoes across the huge space. But nobody answers.

"It's deserted," Emma says, looking around.

The floors are covered in industrial white tiles, and the white walls are spotless. There's a receptionist desk and cubicles all around you, and when you walk forward there's a hallway with a sign that reads:

SEED LIBRARY

PLANT UPGRADES

CAFETERIA

TOP SECRET STUFF

"There must be so many seeds here," you say, looking around.

Emma walks up to the reception desk. "What's this?"

It's a note.

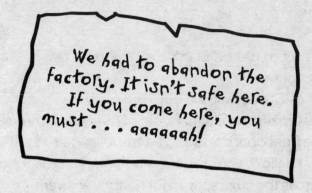

We had to abandon the factory. It isn't safe here. If you come here, you must . . . aaaaaah!

"Who writes 'aaaaaah'?" you wonder.

Emma is pale. "We need to get out of here," she says. She looks around. "Where's Crazy Dave?"

"He probably went to check out the plants," you say. "Let's go down that hallway."

You head to the hallway, thinking you might find Crazy Dave in the greenhouse. The first door you come to is open, so you both head inside. As it shuts behind you, you notice the words "Keep Out" in red on the front.

"Uh-oh," you say.

Emma is gripping your arm so tightly you think she's going to twist it off. You turn to see what she's freaking out about.

The room is filled with round pedestals topped with big glass tubes. Inside each one is a zombie.

"They must have tested the plants on them," you guess.

The zombies notice you both, and start clawing at the glass.

"*Braaiiiiiiiins . . .*" they moan.

Emma rushes to the doors and pulls and pushes, but the mechanical lock won't budge. Next to the door, you notice a control panel with some levers on it.

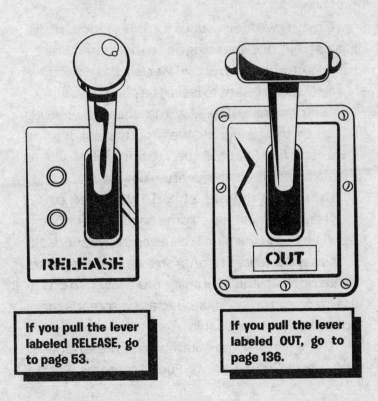

If you pull the lever labeled RELEASE, go to page 53.

If you pull the lever labeled OUT, go to page 136.

Continued from page 110.

"Aaaaaaaaaaaah!" you and Emma scream.

"Twiddydinkies clarfed," Crazy Dave says as he puts a **CLOSED** sign on his shop.

"We're not here to shop for plant upgrades and stuff," you tell him. "Matt ran off, and we're trying to find him."

Crazy Dave looks out of the car window, realizing that the car is speeding down the street. "Sterp!" he yells. "Cabbo no wobble! Plerfs!"

"He doesn't want to leave the plants," you say.

"Sorry, Crazy Dave," Emma says, pressing harder on the gas pedal. "We're getting out of town. If we can't find Matt, we need to find a place where the zombies aren't always attacking."

Crazy Dave shakes his head. "Wiggy womp."

"Hey, you must have some seeds in your pockets, right?" you ask him. "You always have seeds."

Crazy Dave brightens up and starts poking in his pants pockets and searching the seat cushions in the back. You crane your head as he spreads them out on the seat next to him.

There are some Sunflowers, Peashooters, Spikeweed, Sun-shrooms, Fume-shrooms, Potato

Mines, Cherry Bombs, Coffee Beans, Hypno-shrooms, and Magnet-shrooms.

"See?" you say. "Those are good seeds. And there are some night ones too, in case we get attacked at night."

"That is not going to happen," Emma insists, turning to look at you. "This is the part of the movie where we find Matt and then all go driving into the sunset. The zombie-free sunset. The End. *Aaaaaah!*"

She slams on the brakes. You spin around and see a huge horde of zombies blocking the path in front of you. You can turn right on a street just up ahead, or make a quick left onto the field next to you.

"Which way now?" Emma asks.

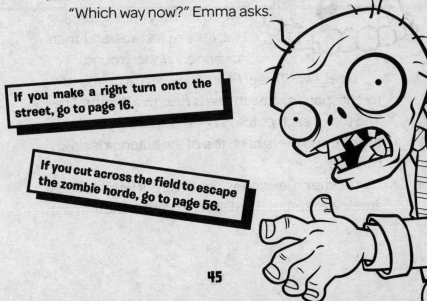

If you make a right turn onto the street, go to page 16.

If you cut across the field to escape the zombie horde, go to page 56.

You grab some Potato Mine seed packets from Crazy Dave and start planting them all over. Potatoes grow underground, so they might be good for zombies that can dig, right?

The first Digger Zombie is munching on a Kernel-pult, the last plant between it and you. But before you can panic you hear the sound of a lawn mower charging up. Crazy Dave has found one and he starts to chase away the Digger Zombie.

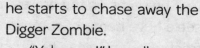

"Yahoooo!" he yells.

Then four more Digger Zombies stumble out of the woods. They start digging with their pickaxes and then disappear underground.

One! Two! Three! Four! They pop up in four different spots, and each one is next to a Potato Mine. The top of each potato's head is sticking out above the dirt, and the light on top of the antenna is slowly blinking.

"Come on, explode!" you urge, but Potato Mines are slow to sprout. The Digger Zombies shuffle past them, taking blasts from the Cob Cannons Emma has planted. By the time the Potato Mines explode, the Digger Zombies are about to breach your last line of defense.

"Run!" you yell.

Nobody argues. You race through the building until you come to a door with a **PANIC ROOM** sign on it. Once inside, you bolt yourselves in.

The room is stocked for emergencies. There are tons of water and canned food, and even a couch with a TV and a video game hooked up.

"This isn't so bad," you say. "We can wait it out."

Emma frowns. "Sure, but for how long?"

Crazy Dave laughs and bursts into song.

"Furzy squirbos whoopee wee, Furzy squirbos whoopee wee . . ."

Emma shakes her head and groans. It's going to be a long wait!

THE END

"We have enough sun for two Tangle Kelp," you reason. "So let's try those."

"Don't forget, that dolphin dude can jump over stuff," Matt remarks. "We'll need to plant a line of defense."

"Oh, right," you say, and you realize you're pretty lucky to have a football player on your side. So you plant some Peashooters on the Lily Pads closest to the zombie, and put two Tangle Kelp right behind them. The Tangle Kelp look like mounds of seaweed, with two evil-looking red eyes shining out from under the leaves. They don't need Lily Pads, because they float right in the water.

You get the plants in just in time. The Dolphin Rider Zombie jumps into the pool, climbs onto his zombie dolphin, and leaps over the first Peashooter.

And that's its mistake. The Tangle Kelp is waiting for it. It grips the zombie with its spindly green arms and drags it under the water.

Matt pumps his fist in the air. "Sweet!"

"Let's get some more Tangle Kelp in there," Emma calls out.

The three of you work together to take down the rest of the zombies that attack the pool. One zombie even tries to snorkel under the plants, but when it comes up for air it gets blasted by a Repeater you've placed on a Lily Pad.

Finally, the zombie wave stops. You collapse on the grass, exhausted.

"Hey, anybody want to go swimming?" Matt asks.

You think of the Tangle Kelp lurking under the water and shudder. "Um, I don't think that's a good idea."

Emma's still trying to get a cell signal. "Nothing," she says. "I bet they gave that part to Darcy Withers. Stupid zombies."

You sit up. "We're in the middle of a zombie attack! Darcy Withers has probably had her brains eaten by now."

Matt looks up at the sky. "Man, it's getting dark already. If they're going to attack again, I need a sandwich."

"BLARF!"

You jump as Crazy Dave runs into the yard, carrying more seed packets.

"Ferg wooper!" he says. "Zombies barfle men-now! Parfern ferg blarg!"

"Oh my gosh, I think I understand him now," Emma says. "A fog is coming, and we need Planterns to light up the fog."

"Gurgle!" Crazy Dave replies, and then runs off again.

By now it's getting dark, so you quickly plant some Sun-shrooms to start generating sun, and some Puff-shrooms. You get some more Lily Pads on the pool. And then you wait. But not for long . . .

"Braaiiiiiins . . . .
braiiiins . . ."

You can hear the low moans of the zombies coming toward you. You're tense, waiting to see what kind of zombie you'll be facing so you know what to plant.

And then the thick gray fog rolls in, and you can't see anything . . . not plants, not the pool, and not the zombies.

"We need a Plantern!" Emma yells.

"But I can't see the lawn," you shout back.

"Just throw it somewhere!" she cries.

So you throw out a Plantern seed, and you wait. And then, miraculously, a bright glow pierces through the fog, and you begin to see the lawn. A couple of regular zombies are shuffling toward the lawn, but behind them you see another one, and it's floating! A red helium balloon is tied around its waist, and it's slowly drifting toward you.

"It can fly right over the plants," you realize. "Emma, what does the book say?"

Emma flips through the pages. "We need to plant some Cactus!" she says.

If you plant the Cactus in a straight line, go to page 30.

If you plant a zigzag pattern across the yard, go to page 103.

Continued from page 43.

You pull the lever marked **RELEASE**, and hear a whooshing sound as the glass tubes in the room lift up. The zombies jump off their pedestals and start shuffling toward you.

"Pull the 'Out' lever!" Emma yells, but the control panel is sparking and buzzing. When you touch the lever, a shock tingles your hands.

"It's fried!"

You quickly scan the room, looking for options. There's a shelf of plants in pots used for testing right behind you. All the way across the room you see two doors. Could they be a way out?

If you grab a Cherry Bomb from the shelf, go to page 28.

If you grab a Garlic plant from the shelf, go to page 100.

Continued from page 99.

The Gargantuar is still reeling from the Gloom-shroom fumes, so you have time to put down two more plants.

"We need some plants with a big punch," you say.

"Squash!" Emma calls out.

"And then I'll follow up with Jalapeño!" says Matt. "I feel like blowing stuff up."

It sounds like a good combo to you, so you quickly plant the Squash. Then the Gargantuar stomps across the roof again.

SQUASH! The Squash jumps up and flattens the Gargantuar. Then Matt throws out a Jalapeño.

BOOM! The Jalapeño explodes. When the dust clears, the Gargantuar is gone.

"Awesome!" cheers Matt, and when another Gargantuar breeches the roof, you know just what to do. *SQUASH! BOOM! SQUASH! BOOM!*

Before you know it, the sun goes down. There's no fog this time—but something much, much worse.

Your whole house starts to shake. There's a creaking sound as an enormous robot crests

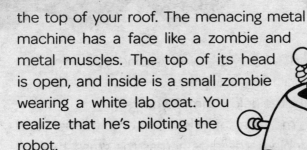

the top of your roof. The menacing metal machine has a face like a zombie and metal muscles. The top of its head is open, and inside is a small zombie wearing a white lab coat. You realize that he's piloting the robot.

"That's Dr. Edgar George Zomboss, the leader of the zombies," Emma reads from the guide. "And that thing is a Zombot. It's a massive weapon!"

The Zombot's eyes start to grow red, and your blood starts to grow cold. That thing is massive. If it starts shooting lasers, all your plants will be wiped out.

Matt's thinking the same thing. "We need a new defense!"

"I'm reading as fast as I can!" Emma shrieks.

You have to make a decision— fast.

If you plant an Ice-shroom, go to page 86.

If you try to counter the Zombot with a Jalapeño, go to page 134.

"Dorf!" Crazy Dave says, and you think you know what he's getting at.

"Take the field, Emma!" you yell.

She makes a sharp left turn onto the field and the zombie horde cuts across the grass, headed right for you.

"Crazy Dave, give me those Peashooter seeds!" you yell.

He hands you the seeds and you toss them out the window. They sprout when they hit the dirt and start lobbing peas at the attacking horde.

"Weebo!" Crazy Dave cheers.

The car's motor grinds as Emma speeds across the bumpy field, but soon you leave the zombie horde behind. On the other side of the field is a dirt road that leads to a highway, and Emma gets on it.

She drives and drives for a while, and there is no sign of zombies. Crazy Dave starts to sing an annoying road song.

"*Niffy noffy wobbly boo! Niffy noffy wobbly boo! Pancakes!*"

You look over at Emma. "So, what's the plan?"

She nods toward the horizon. "The sun is starting to set."

Crazy Dave immediately stops singing. "Yorkle! Zombies!"

"I think he's worried about zombies attacking at night," you say.

Emma understands. "I'll take the next exit."

She drives off the highway onto a deserted road. You don't see any other cars. On the side of the road, you see two buildings, but they look like they've been abandoned: a gym and an ice rink.

If you go into the gym, go to page 14.

If you go into the ice rink, go to page 140.

"There might be people down that road," Emma suggests.

"Or zombies," you say. "Let's just keep going straight."

Emma shrugs. "Fine with me. What about you, Crazy Dave?" But he's got his face buried in *Kittens Ahoy!* magazine.

You keep going down the road, and there's nothing but trees on either side of you. You close your eyes, still sleepy from the night before.

Then—you're not sure how much later—you hear Emma next to you.

"What is that?"

She's slowing down the car as you open your eyes. Blocking the road in front of you is a massive tank. Soldiers in camouflage and green metal helmets are pointing their weapons at you.

You reach in the backseat and shake Crazy Dave.

"Um, I think we're in some kind of trouble," you say.

He looks up from the magazine, shrugs, and then continues reading.

Two soldiers rush the car.

"Out! All of you!" one of them barks.

You slowly get out, your arms raised, while the soldiers look you up and down.

"They're clear!" one of them calls back to the others. "And one has a pot on his head."

A man in uniform pushes through the soldiers. "Can it be?" he asks, and then he rushes up to Crazy Dave and shakes his hand. "I'm General Rootball. We've been looking all over for you, sir. This zombie epidemic is spiraling out of control. The president needs your help to stop it."

You stare at the general in disbelief. "Are you sure you've got the right guy?"

He ignores you as Crazy Dave salutes. "Roffle!" he cries. Then he nods to you and Emma. "Ferns stickie wickie." He wants you on his team.

The general nods. "Anything you need, Crazy Dave. You're in charge of this operation."

"Hmmm," Crazy Dave says. "Tacos!"

You and Emma look at each other as the soldiers hustle you into the back of an armored vehicle. The driver turns back and nods at you.

"Welcome to the team," he says. "Looks like you're official Zombie Fighters now."

"Can you believe it?" Emma asks.

"Not really," you say. "This is all really weird. But I guess being an official Zombie Fighter is pretty cool!"

THE END

You throw a Magnet-shroom in front of the Pogo Zombie. The Magnet-shroom is a tiny purple mushroom with a red magnet growing from the top. There's a whirring sound as the shroom attracts the metal pogo stick. The pogo stick flies out from under the Pogo Zombie and sticks to the shroom.

"Cool! Now it's just a regular slow zombie," Matt says.

"Throw a Squash!" you yell.

Matt obeys, and a big green Squash sprouts. It hops up and squashes the zombie.

"Emma! Are you okay?" you call up to the fence.

"There are no zombies on this side!" she yells down to you. "Come on, let's go!"

"Go where?" Matt asks.

Emma nods to your yard, which is crawling with zombies. "Anywhere but here."

You hate to leave your house, but you know Emma is right. You and Matt follow her over the fence and into the night . . . and whatever is waiting for you there.

 **THE END**

Continued from page 124.

On the seed packet, the Repeaters look like Peashooters, only bigger. The Chomper is a plant with a big purple bulb that opens up to reveal sharp white teeth.

"We should use the Repeaters," Emma says. "If they're anything like the Peashooters, they're probably good."

You and Emma rush outside and plant some Repeaters behind the Wall-nuts. It's a good strategy. When another Pole-Vaulting Zombie jumps over a Wall-nut, the Repeater starts to blast it.

Pow-pow-pow-pow-pow! The Repeater shoots peas twice as fast as the Peashooter, taking down the Pole-Vaulting Zombie.

Then a zombie shuffles up the lawn, waving a flag.

"Is it surrendering?" you wonder out loud.

Matt points. "I hope all those zombies behind him are surrendering too, then."

That's when you see the enormous wave of zombies behind the one holding the flag. Emma grabs the Chomper seed packet and another Cherry Bomb and runs outside.

"Emma, what are you doing?" you yell.

"We need more defense!" she yells back, frantically planting the seeds. Then she rushes back inside and slams the door just as the zombie wave attacks.

You peek through the window at the chaos outside. The Peashooters and Repeaters are battering the attacking zombies with peas. The Chomper gobbles a zombie, slowly chewing it while a Wallnut protects it. The Cherry Bomb explodes, taking down three zombies with it.

When the smoke clears, the zombie wave is gone. You sink back into your couch and breathe a sigh of relief.

"We should call the police," Emma says. She takes out her cell phone and starts pressing buttons. "I can't get a signal!"

You pick up the landline phone next to the couch, but there is no dial tone. The phone is dead. The sun is setting outside, and you start to feel panicked.

"You don't think they'll come back at night, do you?" you ask nervously.

Crazy Dave bursts through your front door. "Zombies garfle wibby woo!" he yells.

You sigh. "He says they'll be back at night. I guess that answers my question."

"This is terrible!" Emma wails. "I'm going to miss my audition!"

You shake your head. "Seriously? That's what you're worried about?"

Meanwhile, Crazy Dave marches through your living room and heads back to your shed. You all run after him, but Matt skids to a stop in front of your refrigerator.

"Need protein," he says, so you and Emma

leave him and go see what Crazy Dave is up to.

"Blarg roggers sun hurfle!" he says. "Wiggy wobble gerfing!"

He just told you that Sunflowers won't work at night, and he thrusts a Sun-shroom seed packet into your hands. Emma picks up another packet from the shelf.

"What do these Puff-shrooms and Fume-shrooms do?" she asks, but Crazy Dave has already taken off again.

"We'd better plant them and see," you say.

You rush back to the front lawn, followed by Matt, who's chowing down on a chicken leg at the same time. You plant the Sun-shrooms closest to the house, and then add some Puff-shrooms and Fume-shrooms.

They sprout just as the zombies start to attack. Some are holding newspapers in front of them. Another one is using a screen door as a shield. But the poisonous puff of a Fume-shroom goes right through the screen.

The shrooms are doing a good job, and then . . . three Football Zombies in full uniform race up to your lawn! Their helmets protect them from the plant attack.

Emma comes back from the shed. "I found this," she says, holding up a book called the *Suburban Almanac*. "It has information about all the plants. It says we should use a Magnet-shroom to get the helmets off the Football Zombies, but I couldn't find any. I did find these seeds, though."

If you use Hypno-shrooms to stop the Football Zombies, go to page 18.

If you use Doom-shrooms, go to page 90.

Continued from page 31.

"We have to go look for Emma!" you say, and before Matt can stop you, you run into the fog.

Something brushes past your arm. A zombie? Then you feel a strong hand on your shoulder.

"Aaaaaaaaaah!" you scream.

"Dude, it's me," you hear Matt say. Then, suddenly, a Plantern is glowing on the lawn in front of you. "I brought some seeds."

The Plantern lights up, scattering the fog, and then you see Emma! She's trying to scale the fence in your backyard, but a zombie riding a pogo stick is jumping toward her.

"What kind of seeds do you have?" you ask Matt.

If you plant a Magnet-shroom first, go to page 61.

If you plant a Squash first, go to page 131.

Crazy Dave is already out of the car and headed toward the carnival, but you reach out and grab his arm.

"That looks like fun, but we've still got to worry about zombies," you tell him. "We should check out that convenience store. We can stock up on supplies and if we get attacked, we can hole up."

Crazy Dave frowns. "Rarfle! Plant-o-rama!"

You try another tactic. "I bet the convenience store has microwave tacos."

He brightens up. "Tacos! *Yaaaaahooooooo!*"

He races into the shop, and you and Emma follow him. The store still has electricity, so the fridges are stocked with cold drinks, and the freezers are filled with microwave tacos. Crazy Dave already has the microwave humming.

You head straight for the back storage room.

"Where are you going?" Emma asks.

"Want to make sure there are no zombies hiding anywhere," you say. You're kind of feeling like an old pro at dealing with zombies, you realize. You check out the room, and it's clear.

When you come back out, Emma is munching

on chips and reading an entertainment magazine.

"This should be a good place to stay for the night," you say.

Crazy Dave starts spinning a rack by the register that's filled with seed packets. "Wahoo! Seedies!" he yells.

He's got the right idea. Before you hunker down, you plant rows of Sun-shrooms, Puff-shrooms, Fume-shrooms, Magnet-shrooms, and Hypno-shrooms around the shop. It's nice to have so many seeds at your disposal.

Then there's nothing to do but wait. You play a game of cards with Emma while Crazy Dave reads *Awesome Beards* magazine. You're just starting to doze off when you hear a familiar moan.

"Braiiiiins . . . braiiiiins . . ."

Looking out the window, you see a wave of zombies coming toward you. But the plants are waiting for them.

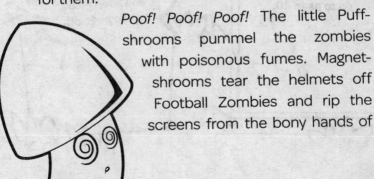

Poof! Poof! Poof! The little Puff-shrooms pummel the zombies with poisonous fumes. Magnet-shrooms tear the helmets off Football Zombies and rip the screens from the bony hands of

Screen Door Zombies. Hypno-shrooms turn the zombies on each other.

When dawn breaks, there's no sign of zombies. "Looks like we made it through another night," you say. "Let's pack up and move on."

You stuff backpacks with seeds and supplies and head out. On the desolate wooded roads, there's no sign of life—or the undead.

Then you come to a road with a sign tacked to a tree: **NO TRESPASSING**.

If you go down the road, go to page 40.

If you obey the sign and keep going, go to page 58.

"Let's blast him with a Jalapeño while he's frozen!" you yell. "For Emma!"

"For Emma!" Matt echoes.

The Jalapeño powers up and . . . *BOOM!*

It hits the Zombot . . . and unfreezes Dr. Zomboss too soon.

"Uh-oh," you say.

The zombie doctor's eyes gleam as he powers up the Zombot again. The Ice-shroom hasn't started to work yet, so there's nothing to stop the Zombot from hurling a fireball at your plants.

You watch in horror as it destroys a row of Cabbage-pults. You and Matt are frantically planting every seed you still have, but more and more zombies keep coming, and Dr. Zomboss won't stop attacking.

You and Matt retreat down the chimney, but Dr. Zomboss and his minions follow you. And then . . .

THE ZOMBIES EAT YOUR BRAINS!

"Well, bombs sound more powerful than peas," you reason. "What do you think, Crazy Dave?"

But once again, your neighbor has vanished. You're on your own.

"Okay, Emma, grab some Sunflower seeds. Matt, grab the Cherry Bomb seeds and follow me!" you yell.

The three of you rush through the house and into the front yard. You can see even more zombies down the street now. This time, you notice that some are wearing orange traffic cones as hats.

"Is that some kind of fashion statement?" Emma wonders.

"I think they're protecting themselves," you say, nervously.

Frantically, the three of you plant a row of Sunflower seeds. The Sunflowers sprout right away. The zombies are almost on the lawn now, so you rush back inside and watch through the window. The lawn is filling with zombies, and your one little Peashooter is doing its best to hold them back.

"Okay, here goes a Cherry Bomb!" you yell, throwing one onto the lawn.

BOOM! It explodes, taking down the zombie closest to it.

But the Cherry Bomb is gone now too, and you only have two left. Will they be enough to hold back the wave?

They're not. You use them to blow up two more zombies, but there are a lot more behind them. Before you know it, the zombies are at your door, pounding with their bony fists.

"We need more plants!" Emma yells, but it's too late. The horde bursts through the door, and . . .

THE ZOMBIES EAT YOUR BRAINS!

"Which seeds should we use?" you ask, panicked.

Crazy Dave looks thoughtful. "Hmm. Eeenie marfle mocha-cha robot dinosaur in the toe . . ." He finishes the rhyme and ends up by touching the Really Awesome Seeds packet. "Ta da!"

"Okay, everybody get in a circle!" you yell, and the survivors quickly gather around you. You plant the seeds in a circle around the group. The Dancing Zombies are slowly dancing toward you . . .

Then the seeds start to sprout. You see Sunflowers, Starfruit, Squash, and Threepeaters.

"Wow, those *are* really awesome seeds!" you say.

Then . . . *poof!* Backup Dancer Zombies emerge from the ground around the Dancing Zombies. There are dozens of disco-obsessed zombies after you now. But the plants are ready.

The Sunflowers keep pumping out sun, powering up the plants. The Starfruit plants shoot in five directions, wiping out zombies all around the circle. The Squash smash

74

zombies left and right. And the Threepeaters let loose with an unending barrage of peas.

"It's over!" someone yells, and the crowd lets out a cheer. Everyone is high-fiving and laughing when Stanley drives up in Crazy Dave's car.

"Hope you don't mind me borrowing your vehicle," he says as he gets out. "We were unable to defeat any zombies, but we did have a lovely drive."

Then he notices the plants and the zombie dust littering the camp. "What happened here?"

Emma steps up to him, angry. "We were attacked, and we fended off the zombies, no thanks to you," she says. "What kind of crazy seed labeling system do you have?"

"It is my own device," Stanley says. "But all's well that ends well, as they say."

The girl you met earlier walks up to Stanley.

"These guys are much better at defeating zombies than you," she says. "I think we need a new fearless leader."

"It should be Crazy Dave," you say. "He knows more about plants than anybody."

Next to Crazy Dave, Delilah beams. "Crazy Dave! Crazy Dave! Crazy Dave!" she chants, and the others join her.

"Silence!" yells Stanley. "There is only one honorable way to decide this."

He reaches into the car and pulls out a big bag marked **TACO TONY'S**.

"We must have a Taco-Off!" Stanley says.

Crazy Dave's eyes light up. "Biggle!"

"Wait a second," Emma says. "You mean instead of hunting zombies you went out and got tacos?"

"That is not important," Stanley says with a wave of his hand. "Now, let us set the rules. Whichever competitor can eat the most tacos in sixty seconds shall become the new fearless leader."

He dumps out the tacos on a picnic table and then removes a stopwatch from his pocket.

"Delilah, please do the honors," he says.

"Blarf!" Delilah replies. "Ready, set, glarb!"

Crazy Dave and Stanley reach for their first taco at the same time. Then Stanley reaches for his second taco and . . . they're all gone! Crazy Dave has eaten the tacos faster than a speeding squirbo!

"*Yooo-delll-aaaa-heee-hooo!*" he yodels triumphantly.

"Crazy Dave is our new fearless leader!"

someone cries out, and everyone gathers around him, cheering.

Before you can join them, a yellow school bus drives into the camp. The driver sticks his head out the window. It's Matt.

"Hey guys!" he says. "Need a ride?"

If you stay at the camp, go to page 125.

If you go with Matt, go to page 144.

You and Emma hurry to the backseat and scoop up the seeds on the floor. Then you plant a few rows in front of the car to protect you.

As you wait for the plants to sprout, you size up the zombies heading for you. Some regular ones, some Coneheads, some Bucketheads, and a few Pogo Zombies.

"Uh-oh, Pogo Zombies," you say. "Better plant an extra row."

Your first rows start to sprout, and you see that they're mostly Sunflowers and Peashooters—not a bad combo. Powered up by the extra sun, the Peashooters start lobbing peas at the attacking zombies.

Wham! The regular zombies go down first, and then the Coneheads. The Bucketheads take a little longer, but you've got lots of

Peashooters, and they don't give up.

You're most worried about the Pogo Zombies, but just as they get close, a row of Sunflowers pops up. The Pogo Zombies jump right over them, but there are plenty of Peashooters on the other side to take them down.

"Got 'em!" you cheer, as the last zombie goes down. You and Emma high-five, and then you turn, but you don't see Crazy Dave.

"Crazy Dave, we did it!" you yell.

He pops up from the back of the car. *"Yaaaahoooooooooo!"* he cries, and you see he's holding a spare tire. "Fargle!"

"And I found something else in the backseat," Emma says, waving a road map. "Now we can find our way home."

You frown. "But how do we know it's safe there?"

"Waffle!" Crazy Dave says confidently, and then you realize it doesn't matter where you go. You'll stick with Crazy Dave and Emma and keep on fighting zombies until there are no more to fight.

THE END

You open the blue door and run through it with Emma at your heels. It's pitch-black, For a minute you're confused. Are you outside? Is it night? Or are you in a dark room?

Then you hear Emma flip a light switch, revealing that you're in a room—filled with zombies!

You turn back to the door, but it locks behind you. Emma pulls on the handle, but it won't open. You're trapped, and . . .

THE ZOMBIES EAT YOUR BRAINS!

"Chuck a Cherry Bomb at the Snorkel Zombies first, since they're closer," you tell Emma. "And then plant one for the Screen Door Zombies behind us."

"Got it!" Emma yells.

It's a solid plan, except that you forget that parts of the swamp are mostly water. When Emma throws the Cherry Bomb seed, there's no Lily Pad to support it, and the seed sinks into the swamp.

"Oh dear," says Stanley.

The Snorkel Zombies are out of the swamp now. You can smell the swamp stench on their bodies. Emma turns around and throws a Cherry Bomb at the Screen Door Zombies behind you, but it's too late, and . . .

THE ZOMBIES EAT YOUR BRAINS!

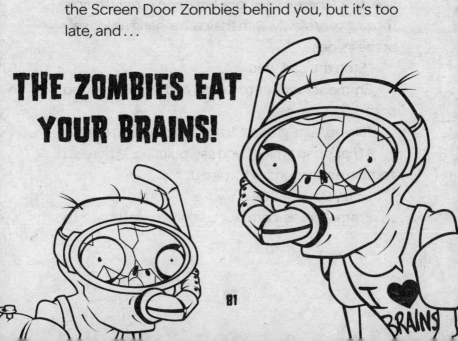

81

"It could be a trap," you reason. "Remember that note the zombies sent us? They were trying to trick us. Maybe they made this sign, too."

Emma frowns. "You could be right," she agrees. "I'll keep looking for the highway."

But the road you're on keeps going and going, and all you see around you are trees. Crazy Dave is snoring loudly in the backseat.

The road turns off into another dirt road.

"There's got to be some sign of life down here," Emma mutters darkly.

You peer down the road. Are those figures you see down there? They look like people, only they're moving very slowly, with their arms hanging loosely at their sides . . .

"Stop the car!" you yell.

Emma screeches to a stop, and you hear a loud *pop!*

"Oh no," she groans. "I think I ran over a rock."

"That's bad timing," you say, pointing. "There's a zombie horde coming toward us."

Crazy Dave sputters awake. "Goober!"

Emma's eyes narrow. "Looks like we'll have to

"stand and fight."

"Unless you have a spare tire, Crazy Dave," you say hopefully.

Crazy Dave shakes his head. "Nopey dopey. Twiddydinkies."

"Well, at least we've still got seeds, right?" you ask.

You look in the backseat, and see that Crazy Dave's seed packets have opened up, spilling seeds all over the backseat and the floor of the car. You can't tell which seeds are which!

"Emma, we've got a problem," you say. "The seeds are out of their packets!"

"Just grab some and start planting! We don't have much time!" she yells.

If you grab some seeds from the backseat, go to page 78.

If you grab some seeds from the floor of the car, go to page 102.

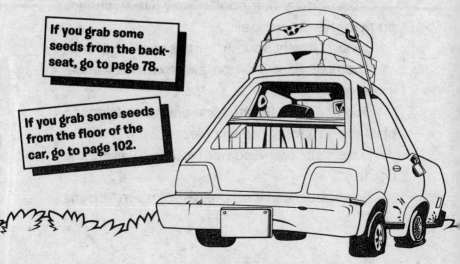

"Hey guys, stand back!" you yell, bursting back onto the roof. You unscrew the cap of the jug, shake it, and then start pouring it on the plants.

"What are you doing?" Emma asks.

"It's Experimental Fertilizer," you say. "I'm experimenting."

All four Gargantuars are on the roof now. Potato Mines and Jalapeños are exploding, Squash are squashing, and Chompers are chomping, but the Gargantuars are still going.

And then . . . *poof!* The plants instantly grow to enormous size! Each plant is the size of a Gargantuar!

"Yooo-de-lay-hee-hoo!" Crazy Dave cheers, pumping his fist in the air.

Squash! A giant Squash crushes one Gargantuar.

Chomp! A giant Chomper swallows a Gargantuar in one gulp.

Boom! A giant Potato Mine and giant Jalapeño blast the remaining two zombies.

"This stuff is awesome!" you say, waving the bottle.

"We should use it on the rest of them," Emma

says. "Come on!"

The three of you race downstairs. Zombies have entered the building, but you use the fertilizer on some potted plants and almost instantly wipe out the zombies.

"This is great," says Emma. "We can use this stuff to take care of the zombies in the testing room too."

"Or we could just get out while the getting's good," you say.

"Proffer seeds," Crazy Dave points out. "Proffer wobbles!"

"Protect the seeds, protect the world," you repeat. "Crazy Dave, that's the most awesome thing I've ever heard you say. You're right. We'll stay here and make more seeds!"

THE END

"Those eyes look hot," you say. "Let's cool it down with an Ice-shroom!"

The Ice-shroom is a blue mushroom with icicles growing from its cap. When the Zombot hurls a gigantic fireball all at you, the Ice-shroom counters it with a freezing blast. And there's a bonus—Dr. Zomboss gets frozen, too.

"Keep attacking!" you yell, cheering on your plants, and the Cabbage-pults and Melon-pults keep lobbing cabbage and melons at the Zombot.

Then Dr. Zomboss unfreezes, and this time the Zombot's eyes glow blue.

"It's Jalapeño time!" you yell, and the angry red pepper explodes, destroying the huge ice ball that the Zombot shoots out.

It's a good strategy—fire versus ice. You keep planting Ice-shrooms and Jalapeños, all the while fending off Dr. Zomboss's zombie minions that are still attacking.

Finally you hear the creak of metal as the Zombot begins to sway back and forth. Your whole house shakes as the Zombot slides off the roof, crashing into the lawn with a sickening crunch.

You, Matt, and Emma rush to the side of your roof and look down. There's nothing left of the zombies or Dr. Zomboss except a twisted mound of smoking metal.

"That's going to be a great final scene in the movie," Emma remarks.

"BLARF!"

Crazy Dave pokes his head out of your chimney. He's carrying a bag of tacos.

"Woggy horf! Glarb!"

You rush over and hug Crazy Dave. You wouldn't have survived without him—or your new friends. You grin at Matt and Emma.

"Let's eat!" you say, and the four of you have a taco party on the roof to celebrate.

THE END

Continued from page 97.

"Hey, guys, stand back!" you yell, bursting onto the roof. You decide to shake the bottle before you open it. So you shake, and . . .

KA-POW! The jug explodes. Luckily, milliseconds before it went off you tossed it across the roof, away from you.

The blast knocks you off your feet . . . and off the roof! You, Emma, and Crazy Dave land on some big leafy bushes below. You're not hurt, but you're pretty shaken up.

"Yahoo!" Crazy Dave yells, jumping up.

"What just happened?" Emma asks, dazed.

"Never mind," you say, grabbing her by the arm. "We'd better get to the car."

The three of you race to the car and jump in. Emma tears out of the parking lot, blasting past the attacking zombies.

"Thank goodness we got away," you say, but you wish things had turned out differently. If the zombies take over the seed company, what hope is there left for the world?

THE END

Continued from page 99.

The Gargantuar is still weakened by the Gloom-shrooms, so you quickly plant two more plants.

"Try a Chomper!" Emma calls out, and you obey. Then Matt plants a Melon-pult in a Flower Pot. It's a watermelon that lobs smaller melons from a vine growing on its back.

"Why'd you do that?" you ask.

"Have you ever seen a watermelon smash?" he asks. "It's awesome. And if it doesn't work, at least I'll get a smoothie out of it."

The Gargantuar stomps forward, and the Chomper chomps down. But the Gargantuar is too big to swallow in one gulp, so the Gargantuar is stuck—but not down. The Melon-pult sends a watermelon hurling at the Gargantuar.

Splat! It smashes right in its face, sending water-melon pieces flying.

"Yes!" Matt cheers.

But it's not enough to take down the Gargantuar. He breaks away from the Chomper and stomps across the roof, destroying all your plants. With no defense, the zombies climb down your chimney and . . .

THE ZOMBIES EAT YOUR BRAINS!

Continued from page 66.

"The Doom-shroom looks wicked," says Matt. The seed packet shows a black mushroom with glowing red eyes.

"The guide says that it can take out zombies in a large area," Emma reports.

"Let's do it!" you say. "Those Sun-shrooms are putting out enough sun for us to get in one big plant."

"I've got this one," Matt says, and he rushes outside and plants a Doom-shroom.

With Matt safely back inside, you watch as the Doom-shroom slowly sprouts. The three Football Zombies charge across your lawn like they're going

for a touchdown. But the Doom-shroom's eyes start to glow, and then . . . *BOOM!*

There's a huge explosion, and when the dust clears the Football Zombies are nothing but dust. There's a huge crater on your lawn where the Doom-shroom used to be.

"Nice one!" Matt says, high-fiving you and Emma. "We blocked that rush attempt. Those zombies won't be sacking us any time soon."

But then you hear the sound of stomping feet, and you see another wave of Football Zombies coming down the street. This time, there are at least six of them.

"The Doom-shroom will get them," Matt says confidently.

But the Doom-shroom is taking a long time to sprout again, and you start to panic.

"Maybe we can plant some Hypno-shrooms," you suggest, but then you look outside at the big crater—you can't plant any seeds in that. And your only hope, the Doom-shroom, doesn't sprout in time. The Football Zombies charge your lawn. They eat all the Fume-shrooms, and the Puff-shrooms, and the Sun-shrooms, and then . . .

THE ZOMBIES EAT YOUR BRAINS!

Continued from page 27.

There's at least one Buckethead Zombie in the general store, and maybe more. You don't want to risk it.

"Head for the swamp!" you yell.

You break into a run, racing for a murky, muddy swamp down the road from the general store. You're not sure what you'll do when you get there, but at least there are no zombies in that direction.

At least that's what you think. Up ahead, you suddenly see snorkels rising up from the swampy waters.

"Snorkel Zombies!" Emma yells.

Stanley looks terrified. "Oh, dear! Whatever shall we do?"

You look behind you. The Screen Door zombies are still coming after you. The Snorkel Zombies will be after you any minute.

"We need seeds!" you yell in frustration.

Emma slaps her forehead. "I almost forgot!" she says. "I picked up some of Crazy Dave's seeds when they fell in the car."

Continued from page 172

She reaches into her pocket. "See? I've got Coffee Beans, Ice-shrooms, and Cherry Bombs."

You know that an Ice-shroom will freeze the zombies for a few seconds, buying you time. It's a night plant, but the Coffee Bean will wake it up. And the Cherry Bombs, well, they'll just blow stuff up.

"Which seeds should we use?" asks Emma.

If you use a Cherry Bomb, go to page 81.

If you use Coffee Bean with Ice-shroom, go to page 128.

Continued from page 137.

"We don't have time to look for defensive plants," Emma reasons. "Let's go grab some of those awesome upgrade seeds."

Too panicked to argue, you follow Emma and Crazy Dave back to the Plant Upgrade room and grab a bunch of Cob Cannon seed packets. Emma grabs some too, and Crazy Dave has Gatling Pea seeds.

Then the three of you run outside and plant rows of seeds on the lawn in front of the building. The sun is shining brightly overhead, and the plants quickly start to sprout.

It's a good thing, because the zombies are getting closer. There are so many of them you can't count. They seem to be coming from the woods across the road. A shiver runs through your spine as you hear that familiar moan.

"*Braaiiiiiins*..."

And then the Cob Cannons go to work.

Boom! Boom! Boom!

The Gatling Peas start shooting.

Rat-a-tat-tat!

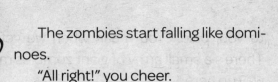

The zombies start falling like dominoes.

"All right!" you cheer.

Then Crazy Dave starts to jump up and down with excitement. "Whoopsie! Lotta zombies!"

Looking outside, you see what he means. Your plant assault is doing great, but there are more zombies coming, and no defensive plants to slow them down.

I should have looked for those Tall-nuts, you scold yourself, but it's too late now.

"They're going to be inside in minutes," Emma says nervously.

"What if we head for the roof?" you ask. "There must be a way up there. We can wait them out and then head for the car."

Everyone likes that idea, so you run through the main room and down the hall until you find a staircase. You run up, up, up, until you open a door and find that you're on the roof.

Lots of plants in Flower Pots are there, soaking up the sun.

"Hey, that's good," you say. "If we get attacked up here, we've got some defense."

Emma peers over the roof and then turns back

to you, pale. "You mean when we get attacked. There's a small army of giant zombies making their way up here."

"Giant zombies?" you ask. Your curiosity makes you brave and you peer over the roof.

Four giant zombies are climbing ladders to get up to the roof. Each one is a mammoth mass of muscle and has a smaller zombie riding in a harness on its back.

"Gargantuars!" Crazy Dave says. "Bargle boogies!"

You quickly scan the plants on the roof. Some Potato Mines, Chompers, Squash, and Spikeweed. All pretty strong plants.

"Will this hold them back?" you ask Crazy Dave.

He shrugs. "Yaaaaahoooooooo!"

At first you think he's just being weird but then you see the first Gargantuar step onto the roof. It stomps on a Spikeweed. Normally, that would be enough to stop a zombie, but the Gargantuar just kicks it off his big foot.

"Uh-oh," says Crazy Dave.

It stomps up to a Chomper next, and the purple plant starts munching on the Gargantuar with its sharp teeth, but the zombie barely seems to notice. And now the second Gargantuar is coming over the wall.

"We need more power," Emma says nervously.

Suddenly, you remember something you saw in the Plant Upgrade room.

"Be right back!" you call out.

Down in the upgrade room, you find a big jug marked **EXPERIMENTAL FERTILIZER**. Fertilizer makes plants grow, right? Bigger plants for bigger zombies. It makes sense.

As you run back up to the roof, you try to read the label, but it's smudged. You're supposed to shake the stuff, but when?

If you shake it after opening, go to page 84.

If you shake it before opening, go to page 88.

"I like those Gloom-shrooms," Matt says. "They can shoot in all directions. I think I have enough money for two."

Crazy Dave is back, so you pay him and take the seeds and Flower Pots he has for you. As you prepare to defend the roof, Emma is frantically looking through the *Suburban Almanac*.

"We need plants that can lob projectiles over the slope of the roof," she says. "These Cabbage-pults should do the trick."

Setting up the roof is tricky. You need to put down Flower Pots first. Then you plant some Sunflowers and Cabbage-pults. Before you plant the Gloom-shrooms, you need to plant Fume-shrooms. Then you need to wake them up with Coffee Beans.

But you're ready when the zombies attack. The Cabbage-pults take down Conehead Zombies and Screen Door Zombies. And the Gloom-shrooms are awesome, bringing down Bungee Zombies that drop from the sky and try to steal your plants.

Then the roof begins to shake, and to your amazement, a huge, hunchbacked zombie appears on the rooftop. It has huge muscles and carries a tiny little zombie on its back.

"It's a Gargantuar!" Emma yells. "And that one on its back is an Imp."

Stomp! The Gargantuar crushes a Cabbage-pult with its massive foot. Then the Gloom-shrooms start throwing off toxic fumes, and the Gargantuar starts to sway a little. The Imp jumps off its back and runs up to the Gloom-shroom and starts chowing down.

"We need a new offensive plan, fast!" Matt yells.

If you go with a Squash-Jalapeño Combo, go to page 54.

OR

If you go with a Melon-pult–Chomper Combo, go to page 89.

"Emma, grab a Garlic!" you yell, as you grab one yourself.

She obeys. "What now?"

You nod to the other side of the room. "Now we get to those doors."

Emma's eyes widen. "Are you crazier than Crazy Dave?"

"Trust me," you say. "I've got a hunch."

You hold the Garlic in front of you and start to run across the room, skirting the zombie horde. A zombie gets perilously close to you, reaching out with its long arms . . . and then makes a face and backs off.

"It's working!" you say. "Come on, Emma."

Emma holds out her Garlic and follows you across the room. A Ducky Tube Zombie stumbles

right up to her, but this one backs off too.

You reach the doors safely.

"How did you know that would work?" Emma asks.

"Well, vampires don't like Garlic, so I figured zombies might not like it either," you say. "Now come on, let's get out of here."

Emma looks at the doors. One is green, one is blue, and neither one is labeled.

"Are we sure these are a way out?" she asks.

You reach for a doorknob. "There's only one way to find out."

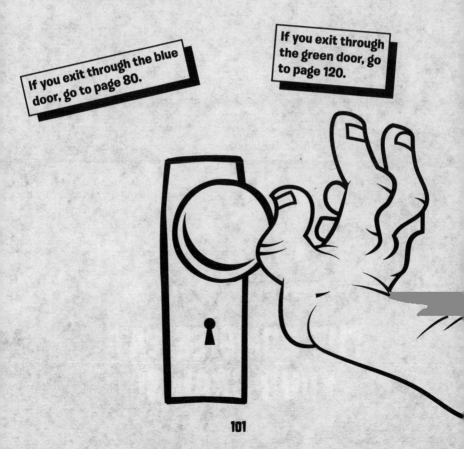

If you exit through the blue door, go to page 80.

If you exit through the green door, go to page 120.

Continued from page 83.

You scoop up some seeds from the floor and plant two rows in front of the car. Then you wait for them to sprout while the zombie horde gets closer.

You can see a variety of zombies in the group: regular ones, Coneheads, Screen Door Zombies, and Pogo Zombies. You hope whatever sprouts will wipe them out quickly.

Then your seeds sprout—and at first you're happy to see Hypno-shrooms. They'll turn the zombies against each other. But it's still daylight, and the shrooms need Coffee Beans to wake them up.

"Keep planting!" Emma yells.

You, Emma, and Crazy Dave scoop up more seeds from the back of the car. A few Sunflowers sprout, but they won't help you with the Hypno-shrooms. Then a brave Peashooter sprouts and starts launching peas, but the one little plant isn't enough to stop the horde. You take off running down the road, but there's no escape, and . . .

THE ZOMBIES EAT YOUR BRAINS!

Continued from page 52.

You take another look at the Balloon Zombie. He seems to be floating in a straight line, but there's a light breeze blowing. Suddenly you get an idea.

"Let's plant some Cactus on both sides of the pool, and on some Lily Pads, too," you say. "Like in a zigzag pattern."

"Got it!" Matt says. "I'll take the fifty-yard line!"

You're not exactly sure what he means, but the three of you manage to plant the Cactus plants in a zigzag pattern across the yard. Then the Plantern goes out, and you can't see anything in the thick fog.

"Let's try another Plantern!" Emma says, and she tosses a seed into the dark fog. You wait anxiously as the sound of zombie moans grows closer—and then the Plantern sprouts, shedding light on the yard.

The Balloon Zombie has floated across the pool already, but that's okay, because you've got a Cactus in its path. The tall cactus is covered in sharp spikes and has a red flower on top of its head. It starts to shoot more spikes from its mouth.

Pop! The spikes hit the balloon, and the Balloon Zombie goes down. Now it's in the range of your Puff-shrooms, which start pelting it.

"That dude is down!" Matt cheers.

Then another wave of zombies attacks, but you're ready, and Emma calls out instructions from the *Suburban Almanac* as new zombies come. The Cactus plants take down Balloon Zombies.

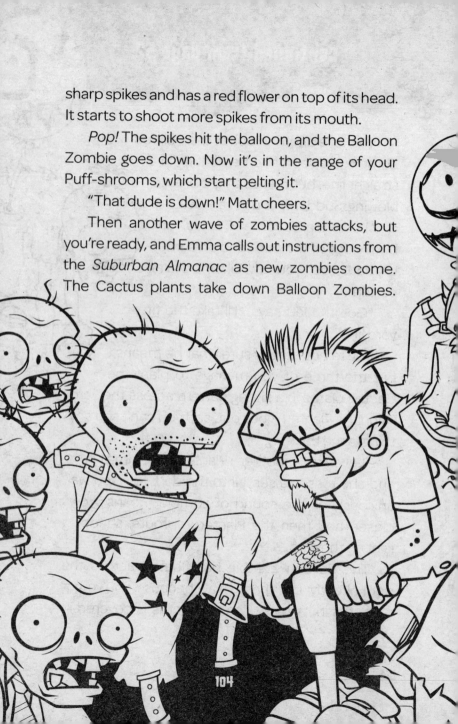

When a Pogo Zombie comes bouncing along on its pogo stick, you plant a Tall-nut to block it. When a Jack-in-the-Box Zombie approaches, you use a Magnet-shroom to steal its dangerous exploding toy before it can blow up your plants.

It's hard to see through the fog, and you keep using Planterns to light things up, and a green Blover to blow away the fog. When the fog finally clears, there isn't a zombie in sight.

All three of you flop to the floor, exhausted.

"I wish we could order a pizza," Matt moans. "I think I've cleaned out everything in your fridge, dude."

"I don't even know how you can eat at a time like this," Emma says with a shudder. "Have you gotten a good look at those things? Those bulging eyes and gray skin . . ."

"I try not to look at them," you admit. "And I sure hope this is the end of it."

"GARBLE MERFING!"

Crazy Dave bursts through your back door, and you see the sun rising behind him. You groan.

"What now, Crazy Dave?"

"Zombies rerf!" he says. He picks up a box of cereal from your counter and starts pouring it into his mouth. "Flerfer pobby noof soddy! Hoggle!"

You brush away a crumb of cereal that flew out of Crazy Dave's mouth. "Zombies are going to attack the roof? We need Flower Pots? New seeds? Do you have all that?"

Crazy Dave nods. "Wabbo woo!"

The three of you follow Crazy Dave outside to his car on the street. He's got a sign on the roof that reads **CRAZY DAVE'S TWIDDYDINKIES**, and the trunk is open to reveal some wicked-looking plants and other stuff. Everything has a price tag.

"We don't have any money," you protest, but Matt pulls a wad of cash from his pocket.

"When the zombies drop, cash falls from their pockets," he explains. "I picked it up."

"Okay, then," you say. "What should we buy?"

But Crazy Dave is running off. "Squirbo!"

"These plant upgrades look useful," Emma suggests.

If you buy the Twin Sunflower, go to page 13.

If you buy the Gloom-shrooms, go to page 98.

"The Squash looks tougher," Matt says. "Let's try that."

Every seed needs a different amount of sun to sprout, and right now there is enough sun being made by the Sun-shrooms for one Squash. You plant it on a Lily Pad and wait.

The Squash sprouts, and it's a green, bumpy vegetable with a big frown on its face. It does look tough! You're pretty hopeful as the Dolphin Rider Zombie jumps into the pool and gets on the back of its zombiefied dolphin. It jumps over a Peashooter, and is headed right for the Squash . . .

. . . but the Squash jumps to the right, away from the Dolphin Rider! The zombie starts to eat the Peashooter in front of it—the only plant protecting you from it.

To make matters worse, more zombies start to storm the yard.

"*Braiiiiiins . . .*

braiiiiins . . . braiiiiins . . ."

For the first time, you're really afraid. What if you can't hold them off?

"I'm outta here, dudes," Matt says.

Emma spins around to face him. "What do you mean?"

"This is a bad game plan," he says. "We're gonna get sacked. The front of the house is clear. I'm going for it."

"But you don't know what's out there!" you yell.

But Matt's done talking. He runs toward the front door. You and Emma look at each other, and then back at the zombies in the yard. The Dolphin Rider Zombie is almost done eating the Peashooter.

"Maybe he's got the right idea," you say.

Emma nods. "We should go after him. I'm kind of worried about him."

You and Emma race through your house, leaving the zombies in your yard behind, and run out your front door.

"Matt!" you yell.

There's no sign of him. But way down the street, you can see what looks like some zombies shuffling.

"I hope he's okay," you say worriedly. "But we

can't go running after him. We'll be zombie chow."

Then you notice that Emma's grinning. She holds up a car key. "Not if we're in a car," she says.

Crazy Dave's car is parked in the driveway next door. There's a sign on the roof that reads CRAZY DAVE'S TWIDDYDINKIES.

Emma runs and jumps in the driver's seat. "What are you doing?" you yell.

"Are you coming or not?" Emma asks.

You don't have much choice. You jump into the passenger seat and Emma peels out of the driveway.

"You can't just steal Crazy Dave's car!" you protest.

"It's not stealing if it's an emergency," Emma points out. "Anyway, what's Twiddydinkies?"

"TWIDDYDINKIES! Blarf!" Crazy Dave yells, popping out of the backseat.

Continued on page 44.

You pull Emma aside. "You know, Crazy Dave has been right about everything so far. We should stick with him."

Emma frowns. "I guess you're right." She turns to Stanley. "Sorry, guess we'll be staying here."

"Disappointing!" Stanley says. "However, I shall not let that deter me."

He points to two of the survivors. "You shall accompany me on this great quest! Let us make haste."

The two survivors unhappily follow Stanley out of camp. A teenage girl with two long brown braids and a red-haired teenage boy walk up to you.

"So, what's up with Stanley?" you ask.

The girl shrugs. "He's a little weird, but we do what he says," she replies. "He knows a lot about plants."

"So does Crazy Dave," you say, nodding toward your neighbor. He's talking to a woman wearing overalls and combat boots. Blonde hair sticks out from under the cooking pot she's wearing on her head.

"That's Delilah," the boy explains. "She wears

that pot on her head to protect her brains from the zombies."

Crazy Dave is smiling like you've never seen him smile. "Squirbos acey!" he's telling her.

Emma nudges you. "Looks like they're made for each other."

Suddenly, the sound of disco music floats across the camp.

"What's that?" you ask.

And then you see the zombie dancing up to the camp entrance. It's wearing a white and powder blue leisure suit, purple sunglasses, and has a fuzzy wig on its head. Its platform shoes are clear, and you swear you can see fish swimming inside them.

"Dancing Zombies!" the red-haired boy yells. "Their Backup Dancers will come soon!"

The Dancing Zombies have surrounded the camp. You run to the car to get more seeds—but the car is gone.

"Stanley must have taken it!" Emma fumes. "That rat!"

"Stanley keeps seeds in his tent," the boy tells you.

You and Emma race to the "Fearless Leader" tent and start digging around. You find a couple of crude seed packets with writing on them. One packet says **SUPER-DUPER SEEDS** and the other one says **REALLY AWESOME SEEDS**. You race back to Crazy Dave with the packets. The Dancing Zombies are getting closer.

If you plant the Super-Duper Seeds, go to page 32.

If you plant the Really Awesome Seeds, go to page 74.

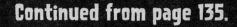

"Dr. Zomboss is frozen right now, so maybe a Jalapeño isn't the best idea," you say. "Let's pummel him while he's frozen."

Matt plants a Melon-pult, a watermelon that shoots tiny melons using a vine growing from its back. "How about a watermelon slushie, Zomboss?" he calls out.

SMASH! The Melon-pult batters the Zombot with melons, and since Dr. Zomboss is frozen at the controls, it can't fight back.

Then Dr. Zomboss unfreezes, and the Zombot's eyes start to glow again. Luckily, you've got another Ice-shroom ready to go.

The rest of the battle is a regular zombie-palooza as you try to freeze and attack Dr. Zomboss while fighting off his zombie minions: Buckethead Zombies, Conehead Zombies, and every other zombie you've seen.

Then Dr. Zomboss is frozen again. A Melon-pult hits him with an exploding melon, and this time, Dr. Zomboss tumbles out of his seat. There's a sickening crunch of metal as the Zombot falls off the roof, crashing to the ground below.

Suddenly, the sun is up, and there isn't a sign of zombies anywhere.

"We did it!" Matt high-fives you.

"But we lost Emma," you remind him. "Come on, we'd better go find her."

"But what if there are more zombies out there?" he asks.

"That's a chance we'll have to take," you say, and you climb down the roof, ready for whatever comes next.

THE END

"I think I've got a Cherry Bomb seed in my pocket," Emma says. "Let's blast our way into the general store and get more seeds so we can fight off these suckers."

"That sounds rather dangerous," Stanley says nervously.

But Emma is already charging toward the general store, and you follow her. Luckily, there's a Flower Pot by the front door, so she plants the Cherry Bomb seed.

"Stand back!" she warns.

BOOM! The Cherry Bomb takes out the Buckethead Zombie lurking in the doorway, and you, Emma, and Stanley run inside. Right by the cash register is a rack of seeds.

"Stanley, what seeds should we use for the Screen Door Zombies?" you ask.

But Stanley is busy stuffing his pockets with candy. "Seeds? What? Oh, whatever you choose will be fine."

You try to think of what you've done already.

"Some Fume-shrooms will penetrate those screen doors," you remember. "But it's daytime, so we'll have to wake them up with Coffee Beans."

"Got it!" Emma says, plucking some seed packets from the rack. "And let's use some Peashooters for good measure."

"I found some Sunflower seeds too," you say.

You run out to the porch and prepare for the Screen Door Zombie onslaught. There are more than you realized, but now that you've got the seeds you need, you're not so afraid. You plant a row of Sunflowers, then a row of Peashooters, and a row of Fume-shrooms that you wake up using Coffee Beans.

"Bring it on!" you yell to the Screen Door Zombies.

They converge on the store, and the Fume-shrooms go to work, filling the air with their toxic gas that passes right through the screens to get to the zombies.

117

At the same time, the Peashooters are in full swing. *Pow pow pow! Pow pow pow!*

When the dust clears, the zombie horde is wiped out—and Stanley is nowhere to be found.

"Do you think he's all right?" you ask.

Emma shrugs. "I think he ran off scared. We should probably try to get back to that camp before it gets dark."

You nod. "Let's stock up first."

You grab a backpack and fill it with seeds and whatever food you can grab. Then you and Emma head back into the woods.

Finding your way back to the camp isn't easy. You plant a trail of Sunflowers and Peashooters as you go to handle any zombies that come after you. It's a good thing, too, because the woods are crawling with them. Newspaper Zombies, Conehead Zombies, and Buckethead Zombies all try to follow you, but your Peashooters take them down.

When you get back to camp, you see a crowd of people gathered around Stanley.

"Those poor youngsters never had a chance," Stanley is saying. "I tried to protect them, but the zombie horde was too strong for even a fearless leader like myself."

"He's lying!" Emma yells, stepping into the crowd, and everyone gasps. "We fought off the zombies while Stanley ran off like a coward."

Stanley nervously taps his fingers together. "I seem to recall things differently."

"Emma is right," you say. "We should have listened to Crazy Dave. He knows more about plants and zombies than anybody."

Crazy Dave smiles, pleased at the compliment. "Gleebo!"

The crowd gathers around Crazy Dave now, talking excitedly.

"Will you be our leader?"

"Crazy Dave! Crazy Dave!"

Emma looks at you. "So I guess we're stuck here for a while."

"Yeah," you agree. "But at least we'll be safe with Crazy Dave in charge!"

THE END

Continued from page 101.

You open the green door, and are greeted by bright sunlight and fresh air.

"We're out!" you cheer, slamming the door behind you.

Emma rushes to Crazy Dave's car and jumps in the driver's seat.

"Still got the key," she says, jangling it out the window. "Come on!"

"What about Crazy Dave?" you ask. "We should go inside and get him."

"That place is crawling with zombies!" Emma protests. "They're probably making brain soup in that pot of his right now."

You look back at the building one last time, and then your survival instinct kicks in. You jump in the passenger seat.

"Let's go!" you yell.

Emma peels off out of the parking lot and races back to the road. You haven't gone far when . . .

"HOOBEE SQUIRBOS!"

Crazy Dave pops his head up from the back-seat. Emma shrieks and almost drives off the road.

"Where are we going?" you translate for Emma.

"I have no idea," you reply, but there's one thing you know—no matter where you go, Crazy Dave will always be by your side.

THE END

Continued from page 12.

"Well, that little Peashooter did a great job taking down that zombie," you reason. "What do you think, Crazy Dave?"

But once again, your neighbor has vanished. You're on your own.

"Okay, Emma, grab some Peashooters. Matt, grab some Sunflowers and follow me!" you yell.

The three of you rush through the house and into the front yard. More shuffling zombies are headed down the street toward your house. This time, you notice that some are wearing orange traffic cones as hats.

Are they getting smarter? Learning how to protect themselves? you wonder. But you don't have time to think. You've got to get those plants in the ground.

You quickly plant a row of Sunflowers across the front of the house, while Emma plants a row of Peashooters in front of them. It's just in time, because the first zombie starts to march across your lawn just as the plants sprout.

Pew! Pew! Pew! The Peashooters start shooting, and the first zombie goes down fast. Then a

Conehead Zombie lumbers across the lawn.

Pew! Pew! Pew! The Peashooters lob peas at the Conehead, but the orange cone protects its head. You're relieved when the cone gets knocked off and the zombie goes down—but this one got too close for comfort.

"There's more coming!" you yell, and then Emma runs up to you, holding a bunch of seed packets.

"We should plant more while there's a break," she says, and the two of you dart outside and quickly get the new plants into the ground.

"Wall-nuts," says Emma, looking at the packet once you are both safely back inside. "I wonder what they do?"

You quickly find out when a zombie shuffles up to the Wall-nut and starts slowly chomping on it.

"It's slowing them down!" you yell.

"I got one of those Cherry Bombs," Emma says.

"Maybe this is a good time to try it."

She throws it at the zombie, and . . . *BOOM!* The plant explodes, taking down the chomping zombie in one bang.

"That was awesome!" Matt says, pumping his fist in the air.

"But it only took down one zombie," Emma points out. "Those Peashooters just keep going and going."

You're feeling pretty good about these plants. It looks like they'll be able to stop all of the zombies. And then . . .

A skinny zombie with blond hair appears. It's wearing a red track suit, sneakers, and holding a long pole in one hand.

"A pole-vaulter?" Matt wonders.

The zombie shuffles up to a Wall-nut. But instead of stopping to eat it, it pole-vaults right over it! Then it starts to munch on a poor little Peashooter.

"No!" Emma yells. She runs off and comes back with new seed packets.

"Will one of these stop them?" she asks.

If you decide to plant a Chomper, go to page 39.

If you decide to plant a row of Repeaters, go to page 62.

Continued from page 77.

"You bet!" Emma replies, climbing onto the bus.

You look over at Crazy Dave. The survivors are trying to lift the big guy in the air, but they're having a little trouble.

"You know, I think I'll stay here," you say. "But good luck, guys."

You wave good-bye to Emma and Matt and start your new life in the survivor camp. Crazy Dave ends up being a good leader. He knows how to save seeds from plants, and when zombies attack, you're always prepared.

And there are good times, too. You find a squirbo in the woods and train it to do tricks. It's so cute! And Crazy Dave even gives you a pot of your very own to wear on your head. It's not so comfortable to sleep in, but at least you know your brains will be safe. And that makes you feel, well . . . glarf!

THE END

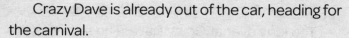

Crazy Dave is already out of the car, heading for the carnival.

"There's no point in stopping him," you say, and you and Emma follow him through the entrance.

It's pretty cool. All of the rides and games are based on plants. There's a Peashooter shooting game, and a Flower Pot spinning ride, and a Shrieking Shroom roller coaster.

Crazy Dave jumps into a big Flower Pot seat. "Poofer!" he cries, and you run over and press the green button on the controls. The ride starts to spin, and then the Flower Pots start spinning too.

"*Yaaaahoooooooo!*" Crazy Dave yells, waving his arms in the air.

Meanwhile, Emma is at the Peashooter game, happily shooting peas at zombie targets. You join her, and then Crazy Dave works the controls while you and Emma ride the Shrieking Shroom coaster. The car you sit in has a cute little Puff-shroom painted on the side.

Click-click-click... the coaster slowly makes its way to the top of the track—and that's when you see the Balloon Zombies. There's a small army of

them floating over the carnival.

"Stop the riiiiiiiiide!" you yell as the car plunges down the track, but it's too late, and you soar through the ride's loops and turns. When you come to a stop, you and Emma look up to see the Balloon Zombies getting closer.

The only shelter in the carnival is a cotton candy stand. Before you go inside you plant some Sunflower and Peashooter seeds, wishing you had some Cactus plants to stop the balloons. It's only a matter of time before the Balloon Zombies will eat your brains . . . but until then, you can eat all the cotton candy you want!

THE END

Continued from page 93.

"Coffee Bean and Ice-shroom, quick!" you yell.

Emma plants the seeds. The Ice-shroom sprouts and wakes up. Pointy blue icicles grow from its mushroom cap. The shroom exhales a breath of cold air that freezes the zombies all around you.

You quickly look around. There's nowhere to run, so you'll have to stay and fight.

"How many Cherry Bombs do you have?" you ask Emma. "And do you have any other seeds in there?"

"I'd love to stay for this discussion, but I fear I must be off," Stanley interrupts. "I'm sure you'll do a good job of distracting the zombies for me while I make my escape."

"Hey, where are you going?" Emma yells, but Stanley has already darted past the Screen Door Zombies and is disappearing into the woods.

"We don't need him anyway," you say. "Quick, throw some Cherry Bombs!"

Emma throws down the seeds, but there aren't enough to take down all the Snorkel Zombies. Half of them emerge from the swamp, dripping with muck.

"Braaaiiiiiins…braaaaiiiiiins….braaaaiiiiiins…"

You look behind you and the Screen Door Zombies are doing the same thing.

"Braaaiiiiiins…braaaaiiiiiins….braaaaiiiiiins…"

"You know, zombies have a pretty limited vocabulary," you quip, trying to cover your fear.

"I really wish Crazy Dave were here!" Emma yells, panicked.

"Yoooooo-delllll-aaaa-eeeeee-hoooo!"

A blood-curdling yodel echoes through the woods. Crazy Dave is crashing through the forest in his blue car, sticking his head out the window and yodeling at the top of his lungs.

"Crazy Dave!" you cheer. You've never been so happy to see him before in your life.

He skids to a stop at the edge of the swamp.

"Glerf wahoo!" he yells.

You and Emma race to the car and jump into the backseat.

"You saved us!" you tell Crazy Dave, as the car barrels down the dirt road, away from the zombies. "How did you know we were in trouble?"

"Stanley nuffle zombies blech," Crazy Dave replies. "Homer saffoo!"

"He says that Stanley is terrible at taking down zombies, so he's taking us home," you translate.

Emma turns to you. "Do you think we'll be safe there?"

You nod to the man in the front seat wearing a pot on his head. He's yodeling out the window again.

"He may be crazy, but I think I'd follow him anywhere," you say.

THE END

Continued from page 67.

You throw a Squash seed in front of the Pogo Zombie, but it jumps right over it. When it notices you and Matt, it starts jumping toward you.

"Emma! Run!" you yell.

She looks over her shoulder at you, and you can see the gratitude on her face. That's the last time you see her, because the Plantern goes out and the fog rolls in again.

Boing! Boing! Boing! You can hear the Pogo Zombie getting closer, closer. Matt keeps throwing Squash seeds, and the Pogo Zombie keeps jumping over them.

"Dude, I can't stop it!" Matt yells.

You stumble, falling into Matt. Only it's not Matt. It's something cold, and clammy, and bony.

"Braaaiiiiiiins . . ."

As the zombies close in on you, the last thought you have is that you're glad that Emma is safe. And then . . .

THE ZOMBIES EAT YOUR BRAINS!

"We need some defensive seeds," you insist. "I'm going to go look for something."

While Emma and Crazy Dave run to get the plant upgrades, you search for more seeds. You don't have to search long. Right next to the Plant Upgrade room is a room marked **SEED LIBRARY**. Inside, you find file cabinets filled with seeds.

You look under "T" and grab packets of Tall-nuts. They'll keep back just about any kind of zombie you can think of. Then you run back outside to join the others.

"I'll plant a row of these up front, and you can put the plant upgrades behind," you instruct. "What'd you guys get?"

"Cob Cannons and Kernel Pults," Emma says.

Crazy Dave holds up packets of Cattails. "Kitty cuteeo!"

"But there's no water," you point out.

Crazy Dave makes a face. "Whoops!" he cries, and then he runs off.

You and Emma get to work planting. The sun is shining brightly overhead, and your plants sprout quickly. When the zombies arrive, the Tall-nuts

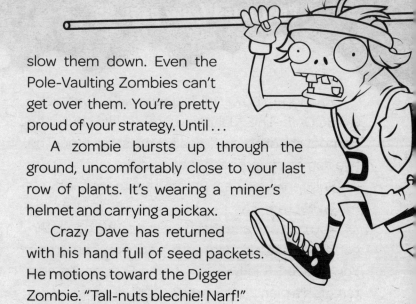

slow them down. Even the Pole-Vaulting Zombies can't get over them. You're pretty proud of your strategy. Until . . .

A zombie bursts up through the ground, uncomfortably close to your last row of plants. It's wearing a miner's helmet and carrying a pickax.

Crazy Dave has returned with his hand full of seed packets. He motions toward the Digger Zombie. "Tall-nuts blechie! Narf!"

You take the seed packets from him. You've got to plant something, fast. Because the Tall-nuts won't stop the Diggers.

If you use Magnet-shrooms against the Digger Zombies, go to page 34.

If you use Potato Mines against them, go to page 46.

OR

You hope a powerful Jalapeño will do the trick.

BOOM! The Jalapeño explodes, but the Zombot shoots out a fireball at the same time. The two flames cancel each other out.

Suddenly, you hear Emma next to you.

"What the—?"

You turn and see that there's a crude paper target on her, stuck there with a suction-cup arrow. You've seen this before, when a Bungee Zombie targeted a plant. But Emma?

"Yeeeee-hah!" The Bungee Zombie gives a crazy yell as it swoops down from the sky. Before you can react, it picks up Emma and then disappears with her!

"Emma!" you yell.

Matt puts a hand on your shoulder. "It's up to us now. We'll get her back."

The Zomboss's eyes glow red again, and this time you figure out that it might take an Ice-shroom to stop the fireball. You plant the Ice-shroom. The blue mushroom looks like it's made of ice, with icicles sprouting from the top of its head. It stops the fireball instantly—and

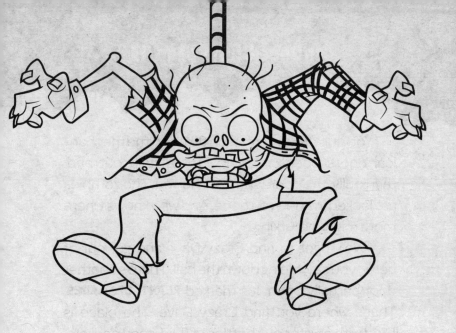

not only that, it freezes Dr. Zomboss!

"Let's take him out!" Matt yells.

You don't know how much time you have. Should you try a Jalapeño now, since the fireball is out of the way? Or would a Melon-pult be better?

If you try Jalapeño again, go to page 71.

If you try a Melon-pult, go to page 114.

You pull the lever marked **OUT**, and the mechanical doors open. You and Emma rush out and, thankfully, the doors shut behind you. The zombies are locked inside—you hope. And who knows where more might be lurking?

"We've got to find Crazy Dave and get out of here," you say, racing down the hall. There's another door partially open. It's marked **PLANT UPGRADES**. That's where you find Crazy Dave. The place is filled with mysterious bottles of fluid, seed packets, and plants.

He's looking at a row of plants in pots on a table. They look like plants you've seen before, only different. Even though you're in a hurry, you can't help but get a closer look.

"Whoa, that Peashooter is wearing a helmet, and it's got four barrels coming out of it," you say.

"Gatling Pea," says Crazy Dave. "Naboo shooteeooo!"

Even Emma gets into it. "Look at this Lily Pad upgrade, the Cattail! It's got a cute

136

kitty cat face and can shoot spikes from its tail."

"That's cute," you say. "But check out this Cob Cannon."

The plant is a big ear of corn with determined eyes that sits on a wheeled cart, just like a cannon. You read the label. "It launches deadly corn cobs. Cool!"

Then Emma remembers. "Crazy Dave, we've got to get out of here. The place is crawling with zombies."

"Yurpee!" Crazy Dave yells, and he speeds out of the room.

When you follow him outside, though, you see that an army horde is surrounding the building. You duck back inside.

"We should use the upgrade seeds to fend them off," Emma says.

"Good idea," you say. "One thing, though. I didn't see any defensive plants in there."

If you help Emma and Crazy Dave plant Cob Cannons, go to page 94.

If you go search for Tall-nut seeds, go to page 132.

Continued from page 31.

"Should we go after her?" you ask.

Then you hear a loud scream in the distance.

"Aiiiiiieeeeeeeeee!"

It chills you to the bone. Was it Emma?

"Dude, it's a lost cause," Matt says. "We have to stay and fight. For Emma."

You nod. "For Emma."

You throw out some more Planterns so that you can see what's coming next—and you don't like what you see. A bunch of zombies wearing miner's helmets and carrying pickaxes are storming the yard.

"Dude, they look serious," Matt says.

You watch as the first Digger Zombie starts digging into the lawn—and then dives into the hole.

"Uh-oh," you say. "How do we stop these guys?"

"I don't know," Matt replies. "Emma has the *Suburban Almanac* with her."

"Well, we have to plant something!" you yell, and you can hear the panic in your voice. But you're not going to give up.

You throw some Starfruit seeds into the fog. When they sprout, the little yellow plants shoot star-shaped seeds in five directions, striking a lot of zombies. But the Digger Zombies are your real downfall.

They dig under your plants, avoiding attacks. You can't predict where they'll pop up. And even though you keep planting Planterns, the thick fog keeps rolling back in, and soon you can't see a thing.

"Let's try this Blover thing," Matt says, and he plants a seed that sprouts into a plant that looks like green clover. The Blover blows away the fog, revealing six Digger Zombies marching right up to your house. You and Matt turn and make a run for it, but they're right on top of you, and . . .

THE ZOMBIES EAT YOUR BRAINS!

"Let's go to the ice rink," you suggest. "I'm guessing that zombies don't like the cold. Right, Crazy Dave?"

"Wompers!" he replies, but you're not exactly sure what that means this time.

Emma parks in front of the ice rink, and the three of you exit the car. The front door pushes right open, but before Crazy Dave comes in he stops and picks up four Flower Pots outside the front door. They may have held plants once, but they're just pots of dirt now.

"I don't think we'll need any dirt in here," you say confidently. "It looks deserted." But he clutches the pots tightly.

Most of the space is taken up by the large, oval surface of ice, which is bordered by a handrail. On the right side of it are the doors to the locker room, and there's a snack bar all the way on the opposite side.

Emma shivers. "It's cold in here," she says, rubbing her arms. Then she calls out. "Hello? Matt? Anybody there?"

In answer, the rink's sound system suddenly

turns on. Organ music begins to play.

"What's that?" you ask nervously.

Suddenly, a red bobsled shoots out of the locker room onto the ice! There are four zombies in red jumpsuits riding inside.

"It looks like a Zombie Bobsled Team," you say in disbelief.

The bobsled is speeding across the ice toward you at top speed.

"Dave, Flower Pots!" you yell.

You quickly set up a line of defense at the edge of the rink. You plant one Potato Mine and three Spikeweed.

The Zombie Bobsled Team lets out a cheer as they near the end of the rink. But your plants have sprouted and are ready for them.

Boom! The Potato Mine explodes, destroying the bobsleds, and the zombies go sprawling across the ice. They skid into the sharp spikes of the Spikeweed plants . . . and that's it for the Zombie Bobsled Team.

"Well, they won't be getting any medals for that run," you joke, and Emma shakes her head.

"Do you think that's all that's in here?" she asks.

"We'd better check," you say.

You scout the inside of the rink, and all is clear. You and Emma push some chairs in front of the front door, barricading yourselves in. Then the three of you chow down on cheese fries, hot cocoa, and hot dogs from the snack bar.

In the morning, you all finish every last bit of food in the snack bar.

"Gobble homer," Crazy Dave says. "Narfle seeds!"

"He's right, Emma," you say. "We should go home. Matt could be anywhere by now, and home is just about as safe as anyplace else out here."

Emma agrees, and you get back in Crazy Dave's

car. She's driving for a while when she starts to frown.

"I can't find the highway," she says.

She goes a little bit farther, and comes to the start of a dirt road leading into the woods. There's a sign tacked to a tree that reads **ZOMBIES, KEEP OUT!**

If you take the road, go to page 36.

If you keep going, go to page 82.

Continued from page 77.

"You bet!" Emma says, climbing onto the bus.

You look over at Crazy Dave, and you know he'll be all right. You decide to go with your new friends and see what happens next.

As soon as you step on board, Matt tosses you a football helmet, and you notice that he and Emma are already wearing them.

"What's this about?" you ask, and that's when you notice—the bus is filled with Football Zombies!

"Whoa!" you cry, quickly backing up.

"Dude, it's cool," Matt says. "If you wear a helmet, they think you're one of them. They made me their coach."

"Seriously?" you ask.

Matt nods. "It's pretty cool. Other zombies don't bother us. And tomorrow we've got a game against the Carolina Gutbuckets. You in?"

"Why not?" you say, strapping on your helmet. "If you can't beat 'em, join 'em!"

THE END